# FIRE IN HIS BONES

Dr. Benson A. Idahosa—a man of faith, called of the Lord—is one of God's chosen vessels, raised up in our generation to declare the Word of God with great power and anointing. My fellowship and friendship with Dr. and Mrs. Idahosa has been a source of much joy, strength and encouragement.

In 1975, it was my privilege to have Dr. Idahosa minister at Evangel Temple. Since that time, God has bound Miracle Center, Benin City and Evangel Temple, Washington, D.C., with cords of love and unity. We are more than friends, we are brothers and laborers together in God's vineyard. We look for ways to help and to be a blessing to Dr. Idahosa and the great work in Nigeria. I have been a guest speaker at Dr. Idahosa's pastoral conventions. The Evangel Temple choir has traveled several times to Benin. We have provided space for Dr. Idahosa's Africa for Christ office here in America and presently there are two missionaries from our congregation serving in Benin City. But we have found that no matter how hard we try to bless we always end up receiving a greater blessing because of Dr. Idahosa's giving spirit and willing attitude.

Words cannot adequately express what God has done for and with Dr. Benson A. Idahosa, but I can say that I know he is a man sent from God—humble, meek, full of faith, courage and integrity.

—*Dr. John L. Meares, founder and pastor,*
*Evangel Temple, Washington, D.C.*

# FIRE IN HIS BONES

## The Story of

## Benson Idahosa

by Ruthanne
Garlock

Scripture quotes not otherwise indicated are from the King James Version.

Quotes marked RSV are from the Revised Standard Version, copyright © 1952, 1971 by the Division of Christian Education of the Churches of Christ in the United States of America.

Quotes marked NIV are from the New International Version, copyright © 1978 by the New York International Bible Society.

**FIRE IN HIS BONES**
Copyright © 1981 Bridge Publishing Inc.,
All rights reserved.
Printed and bound in Great Britain by
Forsyth Middleton & Co. Ltd.
Library of Congress Catalog Number: 81-80951
International Standard Book Number: 0-88270-451-6
Bridge Publishing Inc., South Plainfield, New Jersey 07080
Valley Books, Gwent, U.K.

# Contents

# Foreword

Some people have that "something special" that sets them apart. Then there are the few God sets apart to reach nations—like Abraham, Joseph, Elijah, Paul.

The twentieth century has brought us several of these God-chosen people, but none perhaps has sprung from a more dramatic background than my friend Benson Idahosa.

He first came to PTL in 1976, and since that time he has become a favorite of the American audience. Our viewers have proven faithful in supporting Benson's TV ministry in Africa—the "Redemption Hour," a program that is reaching hundreds of leaders in Nigeria and touching thousands of lives there.

In person, he is a man driven by a desire to reach the world with the gospel. I've seen him electrify audiences—both here in America and when I was with him in Nigeria. God's Spirit rests heavy on him, and the message and signs come in an overpowering, incredible way.

Being with this gentle, anointed man has taught me the awe and respect that Elijah's friends must have known. I feel that for him.

But it's Benson's life story that makes his ministry so

special. Until the book arrived on my desk, I didn't know a lot about his past—that he had been thrown in a rubbish heap and left to die, that he had to endure a grueling, soul-shocking existence as an unwanted child, and that he had to leave his homeland and bride to come to America for schooling.

This book is heart-touching, so the reader should be prepared to "live" with Benson as each page unveils more of his special story. The reader will share the tears and laughter and pain that this book vividly describes.

And don't be surprised if—upon reaching the last page—your own life will have changed some. Benson Idahosa has a way of doing that—in person, on television, or in print.

He is not only special, but specially set apart by God as well. I am privileged to be called his friend.

Jim Bakker
President
PTL Television Network

# Introduction

I first saw him when he walked one day into the classroom of 125 students at Christ For The Nations Institute (CFNI). (The school was only in its second year, and classes were held in a former nightclub.) Someone said to me, "He's Benson Idahosa, our first student from Nigeria."

There he stood, a young black man thirty years of age—tall, thin, meticulously dressed. I watched as he spoke to his classmates. That he was a very intense person was immediately apparent. He dominated the conversation. "A natural-born leader," I thought. I did not know he had once been a sickly infant, left on a rubbish heap to die.

At CFNI he was a bundle of activity. His natural charisma opened weekend speaking opportunities to him that would be denied to the average student. But Benson was not average in any sense of the word. He seemed to carry a tremendous weight of some kind. At times he would weep out loud while a teacher was speaking. What was wrong? Or right? It turned out he was weeping for the souls of lost and dying mankind. . . .

One day my late husband, Gordon, asked me, "Have

you noticed how Benson prays?" I had indeed. "When he returns to his own land, he'll be heard from," Gordon added. Benson felt he just could not take out two years from his Africa responsibilities to complete the course at CFNI, so he left early. Later on, the Institute conferred upon him the Associate of Practical Theology Degree in recognition of his outstanding and far-reaching work.

Before leaving CFNI, Benson shared his vision with Gordon and me: To build a large center and school "like CFNI." (He hadn't told us he had already measured the CFN headquarters building and found it to be over two hundred feet long.) "We'll help you put on the roof," we promised him.

Not long after my husband's homegoing I received pictures from Benson of a huge foundation with walls just started. "What does Benson think he's doing?" I exclaimed. "You don't start that big. I'll write and tell him to cool it."

But the Holy Spirit whispered, *"Leave him to me. Write and encourage him and renew your commitment to him."* So I did, thinking it would be a long time—at least several years—before he would be ready for that roof.

But to my surprise, before the year was out, Benson wrote, "Dear Mom, we're ready for the roof. Come and see . . .!" So on a missions trip to Africa, I visited Benin City. What a sight! Thousands were worshiping in a building that had only huge palm branches for a roof to shade us from the scorching sun. Yes, Benson was ready for the roof. We kept our commitment and sent him $46,000.

That was just the beginning. I know of no young black in all Africa who is reaching millions as Benson is—in crusades with hundreds of thousands in attendance, in his weekly nationwide telecast, in his Bible school, training eager students from several nations. He also conducts campaigns in Sweden, Singapore, Malaysia, Korea, Australia and the United States, where he often appears on national religious telecasts. His burden for souls, his ministry of healing and miracles, even to the raising of several dead, demonstrates he is especially called of the Lord in this end-time revival.

*Fire in His Bones* is the true, fascinating account of an amazing young man—one who is turning millions Godward. This stimulating, yet easy-to-read story is written by Ruthanne Garlock—one of today's finest writers—the former assistant editor of *Christ For The Nations* magazine, and my personal friend.

Mrs. Gordon (Freda) Lindsay
President
Christ For The Nations, Inc.

# Preface

AFRICA. For years I had heard it called the Dark Continent. It seemed so remote—a huge piece of the global map splintered into countries of all sizes whose names seemed to be changing all the time.

I remember as a young teen-ager helping my pastor's wife—who in her single days had served as a missionary in Congo (now Zaire)—when she packed boxes of goods to ship to Africa to her former colleagues. Once she asked me to wear a very matronly looking pair of new black oxfords all afternoon. "Scuff them up on the gravel driveway and make them look worn," she said. "That way my friend won't have to pay the high rate of duty for importing new goods." I never expected to get closer than that to wearing a missionary's shoes.

But then I married into a family of lifelong missionaries to Africa, and suddenly Africa seemed more like a real place. My husband missed being born in Liberia by only a few months. His parents had ministered there as pioneer missionaries. As a child he lived on a mission station in Gold Coast (now Ghana), and as an adult he served for ten years in southern Africa. After our marriage, we completed a four-year mission term at a Bible college in Brussels, Belgium, that is a crossroads for missionaries going to and coming from Africa. I was becoming more interested in this Dark Continent.

Shortly after moving to Dallas, Texas, to work with Christ For The Nations, we began to hear about Benson Idahosa, a former CFNI student. We heard him speak when he visited the school, and he always electrified his listeners. Clearly, a special anointing rested upon this African.

But when a friend approached me about writing Benson's story, I said no. The obstacles were many: I was busy with another writing project; there was the problem of gathering material, and the communication barriers between two people who, culturally, were poles apart. "Don't turn it down until you at least talk to him," my friend insisted.

A few months later he called to say Benson was in Dallas for only one day; he wanted to meet my husband and me for lunch. That did it. Between bites of fried chicken at a corner table in Wyatt's Cafeteria, I was captivated as this man shared what God is doing in Nigeria, and what he envisions for the future in Africa. At the Holy Spirit's prompting and my husband's urging, I agreed to write the story.

But the story turned out to be more intriguing than I had anticipated. The work Benson leads is totally indigenous and totally African. No mission board controls it. The primary explanation for its success is that God is in it.

Fire always attracts attention, and the fire that burns in the bones of Benson Idahosa is magnetic. It draws people—not to him, but to the Lord he serves. He is an energetic dynamo with a single purpose: to take the gospel of Jesus Christ to the lost by every possible means.

Why did God choose a lowly African from a heathen background and give him such a powerfully anointed ministry? Because God almost always chooses the weak to confound the mighty, the foolish to confound the wise. Benson can never forget whence he came, nor can he take any glory for what God is doing through him.

Nigeria is the most populous nation in Africa—with ninety million people. It is emerging as an important political and economic power in today's world. One of every five blacks in the world today is a Nigerian. What better place could God choose to raise up such an anointed ministry?

Benin City used to be called the "City of Blood" because of the human sacrifice practiced there to appease heathen gods. Now the redemptive message of the blood of Christ is changing that reputation. I visited the "City of Blood" and saw thousands of believers rejoicing and praising God because that message had touched and transformed their lives.

Benson believes the world center for evangelism is Benin City, Nigeria. And after seeing the work first-hand, I believe it too.

—Ruthanne Garlock
November, 1980

# FIRE IN HIS BONES

# 1

# A Son Salvaged

It was just a small compound of mud houses like thousands of others in Nigeria. And this day's end was no different from innumerable others. The scorching sun dropped suddenly out of sight, but darkness brought only slight relief from the sticky African heat.

A woman moved noiselessly from a doorway, headed for the rubbish heap about a hundred yards from the compound. Cradling a bundle in her arms, she slowed her steps as she approached the pile of refuse, then knelt beside it. Sobbing softly, she carefully placed the motionless bundle on the heap and hurried back to the house, her black skin making her almost invisible in the darkness.

For a while the faint sound of sniffling drifted from the doorway, but soon only the occasional croaking of a frog broke the silence.

Two or three hours had passed when sudden flashes of lightning streaked across the blackness, and thunder rumbled in the distance. Sheets of water poured from the sky, pounding noisily on the corrugated iron roofs of the Idahosa family compound.

Soon the bundle on the rubbish heap began to wriggle, and the sound of a baby's cry pierced the steady drumming of the rain. Though faint in the beginning, the cries became more shrill and insistent.

The woman's dark form again darted from the doorway straight for the heap now frequently illumined by the lightning. Scooping up the small figure soaked with rain, the woman clutched it to her breast, sobbing over and over, "Benson—my baby! You're alive again—Oh, thank the gods, you're alive!"

The baby stopped crying as the woman loosened the cloth wrapped around her waist, leaned forward and placed the baby on her back, then tied the cloth around both of them to hold the baby snug against her. Hurrying across the compound to take shelter under the kitchen lean-to, she stirred up the ashes under the iron cooking pot containing a bit of leftover gruel and spread the baby's blanket on the ground to dry. When the gruel was warm, she scraped some into a gourd cup and thinned it with water from a nearby water pot.

Carrying the cup of gruel into the house, she knelt down on the grass sleeping mat and placed the cup beside her, then loosening her wrap cloth, removed the baby from her back.

"You're alive, you're alive!" she exclaimed again, hugging the baby to her bare breast as she rubbed him dry with the wrap cloth. "I know you are intended to live—why is it you keep fainting every few days?" The baby's mouth searched for her breast, then he began nursing hungrily with a grunt of satisfaction.

"Oh, my son, I'll never throw you away again, no matter what my husband tells me," the woman sobbed, rocking rhythmically back and forth while the baby continued to nurse. After several minutes, his eager sucking abated.

"You must have some gruel," the mother murmured softly, setting the baby upright on her lap and holding the gourd cup to his lips. "This will help you grow strong."

The baby clasped the cup in both hands and drank the gruel, smacking his lips as he finished.

"Now you can sleep," the mother said, placing the cup on the hard-packed dirt floor and stretching out on the grass mat. She pulled the baby close beside her, covered him with her wrap cloth, and quietly hummed a lullaby. The rain pelting the roof slackened, then stopped, and soon mother and child were sleeping as silence again reigned over the compound.

A few more hours passed before the faint light of dawn crept into the room. The young mother, Sarah, awakened and anxiously checked the baby sleeping beside her. He had no fever, and his regular breathing indicated all was well.

"My son, my son," she murmured softly, stroking his curly head. "I'm so glad you're alive! But what will I say to your father? He will be angry when he learns I didn't leave you on the rubbish heap to die. Perhaps he will send me away as he threatened. He hates you because you are not strong like the other children. . . ."

The baby stirred in his sleep with a slight whimper, then snuggled contentedly against his mother's side. Sarah lay staring at the smoke-blackened ceiling, grateful to have her baby back, yet fearful her husband would turn her out of the house for her disobedience. His angry words of a few days before still rang in her ears.

"That baby is a curse to my household!" John had exclaimed, spitting on the floor. "He refuses to die—yet he refuses to live. The next time he faints, you put him on the rubbish heap and leave him there. I'm tired of your calling me home from my work, crying over a sick baby."

Tears stung her eyes again when she remembered John standing in her doorway and saying with contempt, "He's not worthy to be my son! And if you don't obey me and throw him away, you will no longer be a part of my household."

Without waiting for a response from her, he had disappeared into his own room, leaving her stunned by his final ultimatum. For months trouble had seethed between them, but the conflict over Sarah's fourth child seemed impossible to resolve.

"I know John will be angry when he discovers what I've done," she thought, "but I cannot let my baby die, even if it means leaving my husband and my three older children."

She was jolted from her thoughts when John suddenly burst into the room without warning.

"Just as I thought!" he shouted. "You have brought that worthless baby back from the rubbish heap—that's the crying I heard in the night!"

The young mother scooped the baby up in her arms and scrambled to her feet, backing into the corner of the room.

"He is going to live!" she declared, putting a protecting arm around Benson who was now awake and crying. "How can you throw away your own son?" Tears glistened on her cheeks as she swayed back and forth, patting the baby on the back to comfort him.

"You have disobeyed me," John said sternly, unmoved by her tears. "If the gods meant for this child to live, he would not keep fainting week after week. He causes nothing but trouble in this household. You must throw him away."

Seeing the determination in his face, Sarah realized that for Benson to live, she would have to leave her husband. She started to speak, then thinking better of it, squared her shoulders and looked directly back into John's angry gaze, but said nothing.

"I am going away for a few days to visit my timber stations," he said, moving toward the doorway. "When I come back, I'd better not find this baby in the house."

The baby looked at the angry man in front of him, then cowered against his mother's shoulder, whimpering softly. She shifted the child to her hip and stood silently in the corner, knowing it was useless to argue. John turned and strode from the room, his broad, bare shoulders resolute.

"There's only one thing left to do, Benson," Sarah said with a sigh, putting him down on the grass mat. "We must go away to my people. They will give us a place to live, and you will be safe there." She gave him the empty gourd cup to play with and began gathering her few belongings. "We'll be on our way soon, little one. It's a long journey to the village where my people live."

Spreading a blanket on the floor, she placed on it

some extra clothes, a couple of gourd bowls, some rice tied in a cloth, and several yams. She left Benson on the mat and went outside to the cooking shed, where she stirred up the fire, added a few sticks, and put meal and water in the pot to cook. When the porridge was done, she dipped some into a gourd bowl, leaving the rest on the fire, and came back into the room.

"We must leave a sacrifice for the gods," Sarah explained to her son, as if at age eighteen months he could understand. She placed the bowl of porridge before the juju altar in a corner of the room. "We will ask them to protect us on our journey, and to keep you from fainting."

Benson watched as she knelt in front of the shrine made of sticks and adorned with a carved wooden figure, a monkey's skull, chicken feathers, and some snake's teeth. After prostrating herself before the shrine, Sarah took a piece of chalk and three kola nuts from a jar by the door and placed them beside the bowl of porridge on the altar. For generations the Bini people had called upon the gods by offering sacrifices before such shrines, and praying to their ancestors to intercede for them and protect them. In years past, the Oba, chief ruler of the Benin Kingdom, had often offered sacrifices to obtain favor with the gods. Sarah accepted these traditions of her people without question, as did her husband.

"The juju will see that no harm comes to us, my son," she said soberly. "When you are older, you will learn to make sacrifices to juju, along with the other Bini traditions."

Benson stretched his arms toward his mother, whimpering and smacking his lips. She smiled, picked him up, and sitting on the rough bench near the door, allowed him to nurse at her breast. "It is a good sign that you are hungry," she said, holding his small, black hand in hers. "It means you are getting stronger. But don't dawdle—we must walk to the city to find transport."

Putting the baby back on the floor after he had nursed, she fetched a cup of porridge thinned with water and hovered over him while he drank it. She quickly ate a bowl of porridge herself, wiped the bowl clean, and put it with the other items on the spread-out blanket. She rolled up the grass mat and placed it on top of the pile, then tied opposite corners of the blanket to make a compact bundle.

"It's time we were going," she said, placing the baby on her back and tying him on securely with her wrap cloth. She took a few coins from a jar near the juju shrine and carefully tied them in a cloth, then tucked them safely in the folds of her wrap cloth.

"We must try to reach your grandmother's house before sundown," she said, still talking to the baby as if he understood everything perfectly. "When your father comes home he will be rid of the baby he despises, but he will also be rid of his senior wife. I'll leave the older children here; your father and his other wife will see that they are cared for."

She stooped to pick up the bundle of belongings, surveyed the room once again, then went out the door, pulling it shut with an air of finality. The eastern sky was red with a glorious sunrise which reflected in the puddles left from the rain of the night before. No one was yet astir in the Idahosa compound; John had already left by bicycle to go to his timber station. Sarah moved quietly and unnoticed between the buildings to the nearest road.

She stopped, lifted the bundle to her head and deftly balanced it there so her hands were free, then set off toward the business district of Benin City, her strong body moving rhythmically with the load. Benson looked with wide eyes at the bright-red, flamboyant blossoms on the trees by the roadside, and other women sauntering along with baskets of grain, yams or fruit on their heads. Even at this early hour, roadside vendors were huckstering bananas, pawpaws, loaves of bread and handmade wares of every description.

With the warmth of his mother's body against his and the gentle motion of her movements, Benson's eyelids grew heavier and heavier, and he was soon asleep. After an hour's walk, Sarah reached the transport station where she paid the fare for passage to Ewasso, her family's village, and climbed on the back of the old truck along with a dozen other passengers. She untied the baby from her back and cradled him on her lap as she sat on the floor of the truck bed, her bundle beside her.

"I know I'm doing the right thing," she thought as she bumped along on the three-hour journey, "but it won't be easy to ask my family to take me and Benson into their household; they have so many mouths to feed already. But I'll help with the farming—sell produce in the market—whatever I have to do to provide for my son." She looked down at Benson sleeping contentedly, his dark lashes curled against his smooth, brown cheeks. "I don't know what it is," she mused, rocking him gently, "but this son seems special somehow—he is different from the others. . . ."

# 2

# A Son Rejected

A planting season and a rainy season had passed in the tiny farming village of Ewasso. Sarah and little Benson seemed to flourish in her parents' home, where they were free from the constant discord of the Idahosa household. Benson was still frail and occasionally susceptible to illness, but soon his fainting spells had diminished, and finally they had stopped altogether.

One afternoon Sarah was sitting in the shade of a mango tree, watching the children play, glad for a respite from the tropical sun. Her back ached from working in the yam harvest most of the day, and she welcomed the chance to rest. She noted with pride that Benson was as tall as the other children who were two and a half or three years old, and he appeared healthier than she had seen him for months.

"Surely your father would be proud if he could see you now," she mused as the youngsters laughed and shrieked at one another. "He would be glad I did not leave you to die on the rubbish heap."

Sarah looked up toward a man walking in her direction, and was stunned. It was her husband! "John, what are you doing here?" she asked, jumping to her feet in shocked surprise.

"I had to visit a timber station not far from here," he answered. "And I thought I'd just come by and see how you're getting along."

"I'm doing fine—and Benson is healthier than he's ever been," she said, nodding toward the group of youngsters nearby. Then she had her own question. "How are the older children?"

"They are well—the two oldest are in school now—"

"Mama—Mama," Benson called, running toward Sarah and grabbing her around the knees. She picked him up and perched him astride her hip.

"This is your son Benson," she said to John proudly. The toddler looked at the stranger with a solemn gaze, then hid his face shyly against his mother's shoulder. "Won't you stay and have a meal with us?" Sarah invited.

"Yes, thank you," John replied, a hint of a smile on his stern face. "It's been a long time since you've prepared a meal for me. I've not forgotten your pepper stew."

"You can visit with my father until the food is ready," she said, bowing to touch one knee to the ground. "I'll go help with the cooking." She crossed the yard to the cooking shed and put Benson down to play nearby where she could keep an eye on him. "That's your father who has come to visit us!" she said excitedly. "And he's staying for supper!"

The unexpected reunion with John went well that evening, and he ended up staying overnight. About three weeks later he was back again, and thereafter his visits became more frequent. The months of separation seemed to have softened the animosity between them, but Sarah made only casual references to Benson so as not to stir up the old argument.

After several weeks had passed, Sarah realized she was pregnant with her fifth child. On learning this, John urged her to return to his household, but she was reluctant to do so. Because of her great affection for Benson and John's continued indifference toward the child, Sarah preferred to stay with her parents, though John continued to visit often. But finally, after the baby was born and Benson had become four years old, John convinced her to move to his compound at Agbo, a village near the timber station where he was currently working.

Sarah resumed her wifely duties, and over the next several years bore additional children, but Benson continued to hold a special place in her heart. John, although pleased that Sarah had returned, was greatly absorbed in his work as a timber contractor and in his duties as the high priest of juju for the Idahosa family. By custom he was responsible for teaching the tradition to his first son—Benson's older brother—so that child received more attention from him than any of the others.

In the years that followed, Benson grew stronger and healthier under the watchful care of his mother. When he was eight years old, she convinced John to pay the fifteen-cents-a-month fee so she could enroll the youngster in the Anglican mission school at the edge of their village. Every morning Benson trooped off down the footpath with his older brothers and sisters, and began learning this strange language called English that all the white school teachers spoke.

Attending school stimulated Benson as nothing else had done in his mostly mundane existence. He found it exciting to begin learning a new language, and to discover that the pages of a book could speak to him. The opportunity to learn revived his spirit as his mother's attentive care had restored his health, and he quickly became one of the top pupils in his class.

But Benson's excursion into the world of learning was short-lived. After only one year of school, his father moved again to establish another timber station. This time the children were not able to go to school because John was uncertain how long his job would last at that location. The next year brought still another move—this time to Ewasso, the village of Sarah's parents—and here Benson soaked up a second year of study in another Anglican mission school. He was disappointed when the school term came to a close, and life took on the everyday sameness again.

One morning Benson (who was now eleven years old)—and the younger children—were helping Sarah gather the laundry. They were about to head for a nearby stream where they would all bathe and then wash their clothes, when John suddenly appeared in the courtyard and summoned Benson.

"I wonder what he wants?" Benson thought, dropping the bundle of laundry and scampering across the courtyard. "Father hardly ever even speaks to me—I wonder if he is about to punish me. . . ."

John motioned and Benson followed him to his

quarters where two strangers were waiting. The boy looked from one face to the other, bewildered as to what all this meant, and feeling very uneasy.

"Son, these are men who work for my brother Joseph who lives in Igbanke," John said in a very businesslike tone. "I am sending you to live with your Uncle Joseph to work on his farm—these men have come to take you there."

Benson stood rooted to the spot, stunned by the unexpected news. He was about to ask a question when his father continued. "When I was a boy, my father sent me away to work on a farm," he explained. "I feel one of my sons should have the same experience I had."

In Benson's mind the question screamed, "Why me, Father?" But he remained silent, staring at the floor and scraping his toe in the dirt. He longed desperately to feel close to this aloof man who was his father, but it seemed there was an inpenetrable wall between them.

"Go get your things together," his father said brusquely. "You'll be leaving right away—don't keep these men waiting."

"Yes, Father," Benson answered in a barely audible voice, retreating from the room and walking slowly back across the courtyard. Sarah and the children were waiting impatiently to begin their trek to the river.

"What is it, Son?" his mother asked, puzzled by his somber face and the hurt look in his eyes.

"Come in here," Benson answered, stepping inside their quarters and sinking down on the battered bench by the door. "Father is sending me away," he said bluntly. "I'm to go live in Igbanke with Uncle Joseph and work on his farm. Two of his men are here to take me with them—I must leave right away."

They both sat staring at the juju shrine across the room as the significance of those words sank in. It would mean separation from his mother, who had such a great affection for him. He would be living with people he had never even met, and he would be expected to do the work of a man.

"Why is he doing this?" Benson asked, searching his mother's face. "Why does he want to get rid of me?"

"I don't know, Son," she replied, shaking her head. "Your father and I have had many problems. Perhaps he has never forgiven me for disobeying him and retrieving you from the rubbish heap when you were a baby."

Sarah put her arm around his shoulder and drew him close, silent tears coursing down her cheeks and wetting his woolly hair. "I suppose he is taking his anger out on you, but it seems so unfair—"

"I must not keep the men waiting," Benson said, nervously jumping to his feet. "Father sent me back only long enough to get my things together. What shall I take with me to Igbanke?"

Sarah brushed away the tears with the back of her hand. "I want you to take the grass sleeping mat I made for you—at least that will remind you of home," she answered, fetching the mat from the corner of the room. "I'll get your clothes from the laundry bundle outside."

Within minutes Benson's few worldly possessions were tied in a small bundle he could carry on his head.

---

"I'll pray for you and make juju sacrifices for your safety, Benson," she said as he was about to go out the door.

Benson stopped and looked back at the shrine and then at his mother. "I have no interest in juju," he said, "and I don't believe your gods hear your prayers. But don't worry about me; I'll be okay."

"Benson, Benson—Father is calling for you," one of the children yelled, running up to the doorway.

"I must go," Benson said, dry-eyed and resolute. "Goodbye, Mother." With that he was gone.

It was a hot and dusty four-hour ride to Igbanke on the back fender of an old bicycle. One man pedaled the bike on which Benson rode, and the other followed on another bicycle carrying the bundle of belongings. The men accompanying Benson paid little attention to him, so he was left to speculate as to why this was happening, and what his new life might be like.

Perhaps this was his father's way of repaying a debt to Uncle Joseph. It could be that John Idahosa simply wanted one less mouth to feed, or perhaps he resented the fact that this son of his showed no interest in learning the rudiments of juju worship. Whatever the reason, the result was the same—Benson must work as a servant for as long as his father compelled him to, and for the time being, his master would be Uncle Joseph.

"I wonder if my uncle will let me go to school?" Benson mused. He wanted more than anything else to be able to get an education; his scant two years of schooling had only whetted his appetite. He must find a way to continue.

---

With some trepidation, Benson followed the guardians up the path to meet his uncle, who came out of his thatch-roofed hut to greet them as they approached the compound. "Ah, so you must be John's son Benson," the man said, extending his hand.

"Yes, sir," Benson replied, grasping his hand and kneeling to touch one knee to the ground—the traditional tribal gesture of showing respect for one's elders. He desperately hoped his nervousness did not show.

"Your father says you don't know much about farming," Uncle Joseph said. "Guess we'll have to teach you. I hope you'll make a good worker—this is a big farm."

The guardians departed, and Benson followed Uncle Joseph to the courtyard of the compound, carrying his bundle awkwardly beside him. One of the wives who was tending the cooking pot gave him a bowl of red pepper stew—most welcome after the journey.

Then he met the cousins with whom he would share the home. They were all younger than he, and they seemed to like Benson immediately. To these farm youngsters, he was the older and wiser cousin and they looked on him with respectful awe. Benson finished his stew, then Uncle Joseph showed him where he would be sleeping.

Despite his youth and frailty, the sowing and harvesting of groundnuts, yams, cassava, okra and other crops quickly became part of Benson's workaday world. At first his muscles ached from the unaccustomed work, and he rubbed blisters on his hands from wielding a cutlass and a hoe. But soon his back and shoulders grew stronger from the daily exertion.

Besides doing field work, he served as "houseboy." He gathered and chopped firewood for Uncle Joseph's two wives, hauled water from the river nearby, and kept the mud-packed floors and courtyard swept clean with a homemade straw broom. At night he spread his grass mat and slept on the floor of the main room of his uncle's hut.

In the evenings after supper, Benson's cousins played games until dusk, and they often begged him to join them. He would sometimes respond by teaching them a new game, or telling them a story. Their favorite was the tale about Ehenua, one of Benson's ancestors from five generations back.

Ehenua was a special guard for the *Iyase* (Edo word for "premier") of the Benin Kingdom. Iyase-Node held the highest office in Benin, appointed by the *Oba* (king), Osemwende. To help him in ruling such a vast territory as the Benin Kingdom, the Oba appointed many chiefs over the numerous villages, and all these chiefs together made up the Oba's council. Iyase-Node, as chairman of the council and commander-in-chief of the Benin warriors, was a very powerful man. He had so much power, in fact, that he became very proud of his own position, and very jealous of the Oba.

Late one night, Iyase-Node received a mysterious visit from a junior chief who lived in a nearby village. Ehenua, whose duty it was to guard the private quarters of Iyase-Node, overheard their conversation. He was most disturbed to hear that his master was plotting to overthrow the Oba and take over the kingdom, with the help of some lesser chiefs who wanted more power than the Oba had been willing to give them.

The knowledge of this devious plot put Ehenua in a very precarious position. Should his master learn that he knew of the plot, Ehenua's life would be in danger. However, if the Oba were to find out about the plot, he could order Iyase-Node's murder, as well as the murder of his guards and servants. That meant Ehenua would die.

But loyalty to the Oba is a deeply ingrained tradition of the Edo people of Benin, so Ehenua went to the Oba and reported the plot. Because Ehenua worked so closely to Iyase-Node, the Oba appealed to him to defend the throne by murdering the traitorous premier. Within a few days, Ehenua saw his opportunity. Stealthily he crept up behind the premier, then thrust him through with a spear.

To express his gratitude, the Oba bestowed a special title upon Ehenua *(Ezomo,* meaning second in command to the premier of Benin) and gave him the honor of wearing the treasured coral beads, which only royalty was normally permitted to wear. Also, Ehenua's wives were permitted to dress like the Oba's wives—with coral beads and elaborate headdresses—a privilege normally forbidden to common citizens.

"And from that day to this," Benson would conclude with a flourish, "a member of the Idahosa family has always served as *Ezomo* in the Oba's palace with the highest respect of the king."

One evening after a hard day's work of hoeing beans and chopping firewood, Benson sat leaning against the mud brick wall of his uncle's house, watching the crimson sunset. The children called to him to join them at play, but he was too tired to move, so he watched from a distance.

"We're playing school, and I'm the teacher," the oldest girl shouted. "Father says we're to start school tomorrow!"

Excitement surged through Benson at the thought of being able to go to school. His weariness suddenly seemed to evaporate. When he stretched out on his grass mat that night he could hardly sleep as he envisioned himself sitting in a classroom in the village school, learning the contents of the fascinating books he had seen. If only he could go to school again, it would be worth all his back-breaking work on the farm.

Earlier than usual the next morning, Benson was up tending to his duties around the compound. When he was sure the women had plenty of firewood and water for cooking, he used a gourd to dip from the pot of rain water, washed himself, then donned clean clothes. About the time Uncle Joseph was finishing his breakfast, Benson approached him where he was sitting in the courtyard just outside his door.

"Uncle Joseph," he began hesitantly, "the children told me last night that the village school opens today.

---

May I go with them to school, please, sir?"

He stood at attention, scarcely breathing, studying his uncle's inscrutable face. Joseph finished drinking from his gourd cup and put it down on the ground. "You don't understand, boy," he replied, shaking his head. "Your father sent you here to learn farming, not to go to school."

Benson looked at him incredulously, then dropped his head, trying not to show his disappointment.

"Farmers don't have to know how to read and write," his uncle continued, "and I can't afford to pay any more school fees. Besides, you and I will be staying out in the bush for many weeks to do some trapping as soon as the *Igue* festival is over. There is no time for school."

Benson could not believe what he was hearing. If Uncle Joseph would not allow him to go to school, then all his hard work was in vain!

"Is it possible that my father could pay my school fees, and that I could start when we come back from the bush?" the boy asked, grasping for a straw of hope.

"Your father sent you here to farm, not to go to school," Joseph repeated impatiently, getting to his feet. "You can't learn farming with your nose in a book! Now hurry up and get to the field. I want you to finish the bean harvest today."

Joseph crossed the courtyard to bid goodbye to his children who were about to depart for school, and left the stricken boy standing dumbfounded and dejected.

Benson walked slowly to his quarters, took off his clean clothes, folded them carefully and put them away. Then he put on a ragged pair of knickers to wear in the field. He slaved all day picking beans, rivulets of perspiration pouring off his body. But as he worked, his mind was busy devising a plan. By late afternoon he finished the last row, and carrying a huge basket of beans on his head, started home with a look of determination on his face.

"If Uncle Joseph won't let me go to school, I'll have to find some other way to learn," he reflected. "But I'm determined not to be a farmer for the rest of my days—there's got to be more to life than picking beans or harvesting yams."

# 3

# A Thirst for Learning

Since school had started, Benson's cousins no longer had time to while away their evenings playing games. They had lessons to write and arithmetic problems to cipher. Instead of chattering in their native Edo language, they were required to practice speaking and writing English—the official language in Nigeria since the British had taken over the government around 1900.

Now Benson rose earlier and worked even harder to be sure his chores were finished by supper time. The high point of his day was in the early evening after supper. His cousins would sit in the courtyard, their school books spread on the ground around them, reciting the lessons they had had at school that day. And Benson would sit with them. This was his classroom, his chance to learn, and he made the most of it. Although they knew Benson was a servant—without the privileges they enjoyed as sons and daughters—the children loved him dearly and delighted in helping him to learn.

The eager scholar worked on the lessons at every opportunity with dogged determination, and soon had passed the most advanced pupil among his young cousins. To prepare for examinations the children would quiz one another, and Benson always got more correct answers than anyone. It become a game to see who could come closest to getting as many answers right as the boy who wasn't even enrolled in school.

The weeks rolled by, and soon it was Christmas time. Though the season's Christian significance meant nothing to those Bini people who practiced juju worship, their own *Igue* festival was a time of ceremonial dancing, exchanging of gifts, and making offerings of goats, chickens and kola nuts to the juju gods of good luck. For a Bini, this was the time-honored tradition of thanking the gods for their protection during the previous year. Benson's cousins were high with anticipation, for their father always bought them new clothes at this time of year.

One day while the children were at school, Uncle Joseph came home from market with a large bundle which he carried into his hut. Benson was sweeping the courtyard outside when he heard his uncle calling him. He went over to the door of Joseph's hut and looked in to see piles of new clothes for his cousins stacked on a bench.

"Look, Benson," the older man said, holding up a simple white cotton undershirt from the top of the pile. "I bought you this singlet at the market today. If you do your work well, I'll give it to you for Christmas."

"Yes, sir—thank you," Benson stammered, a bit bewildered. "I'll do my best, sir." He had never received a Christmas gift before, so he hardly knew what to say.

He went back to his sweeping and household chores, trying harder than ever to please his master. He knew that if it appeared he was shirking his duties he might be denied the privilege of studying with his cousins after supper at night. And that privilege was more precious to Benson than any new shirt.

At last the long-awaited festival day dawned, and the children squealed with delight when they received their new clothes. "Benson, look!" one of the boys shouted, running over to where Benson was chopping firewood to fuel the fire under the cooking pots. "See my new suit!" He strutted back and forth to show off his bright blue jacket and trousers with a checkered shirt. "I even got new shoes," he said proudly, pulling up his trouser leg so Benson could see the shiny leather and his bright red socks.

"That's very nice," the older boy answered with a grin. "You look super."

Benson stacked the wood in a pile, wrapped a cord around it, and carried it to the cooking shed in the courtyard. The place hummed with activity—the women preparing rice, yams and pepper stew with beef, and the children chattering and singing, eagerly awaiting the guests expected to arrive any minute. Benson put down the load of wood, picked up an empty calabash and started out of the courtyard to fetch water when he almost bumped into Uncle Joseph.

"Good morning, sir," he said politely.

"Benson," Uncle Joseph growled, "I was just out looking over the yam plots yesterday. Lots of weeds growing there—I expected that weeding to be finished by now. What's the matter with you?"

Benson drew back as if he had been struck. "I'm sorry,

sir," he replied, "But with guests coming for the feast day, the women have had extra work for me here on the compound. But I'll begin work on the weeding tomorrow. . . ."

"Well, I think you've just been spending too much time with those books and neglecting your work," the man complained. "I've decided not to give you that new shirt, after all." Without waiting for a response, he strode across the courtyard and began greeting the arriving guests.

Benson stood speechless, a sick feeling in the pit of his stomach. Thoughts filled with ache churned in his mind. "I was never able to please my father, and I guess I'll never be able to please Uncle Joseph, either," he lamented. "But someday when I'm old enough, I'll get a job and buy a whole suit of clothes for myself. Maybe I'll even buy a new suit for Uncle Joseph. Maybe then he would be pleased with me. . . ."

With slower steps he continued his trek to the river to fetch water, deep in thought. He dipped the calabash into the river to fill it, balanced it on his head, and trudged back to the compound, his bare feet pounding the worn dirt path. Looking at his own ragged clothes and remembering his cousin's new suit and shoes, he wondered what it would be like to be able to dress like that. He had never worn a pair of shoes in his life; the few old clothes he owned were things his mother had sent him. He had looked forward to getting a brandnew shirt, even if it was only a singlet. But he was much more distraught over his uncle's disapproval than over the fact he would not get the shirt.

Back at the compound, the festivities were under way, with drums beating, children shouting and dancing, and palm wine flowing. But for Benson the joy had gone out of the day. When the food was served he took a bowl of rice and pepper stew and retreated to a quiet place away from the courtyard to eat in solitude.

He felt a stab of homesickness for his mother and the familiar Idahosa compound, but he refused to indulge in the futility of crying over it. Instead, he finished his meal, then walked to the yam plots and began the endless task of pulling weeds. But as he worked, he recited the addition and subtraction tables he had learned with his cousins the week before.

A few days after the end-of-year festivities, Uncle Joseph reminded his young trainee that it was time for their hunting trip. To the book-hungry boy this was not good news. It meant just one thing: no more lessons with his cousins each evening. But Benson knew that to protest would be futile, and he had no one to whom he could talk and air his frustration. So he quietly went about gathering the provisions they would need for the excursion.

By early afternoon everything was ready and the two set off. They trekked single file, Benson a few steps behind his uncle, with the sleeping mats, cooking pot, and a bundle of food balanced on his head. Soon the familiar sounds of the village were behind them. The thick growth of the bush had almost obliterated the narrow path they followed, forcing the slender boy to dodge the twigs and branches while at the same time keeping his head load in place. The sounds of chattering monkeys and birdcalls echoed in the trees overhead and grew louder as they went deeper into the bush.

After walking for more than an hour through the shoulder-high grass and towering gum trees, they came to a clearing. Here Uncle Joseph had built a small mud hut which he used each year during trapping season. This would be their home over the next several weeks. Benson set to work making a broom of twigs to sweep out the hut. He spread their sleeping mats on the ground inside, cut a supply of firewood, and hauled water from a nearby stream. Then he gathered kola nuts that had fallen from the trees at the edge of the clearing; the chestnut-shaped nuts would be their staple food while they worked in the bush in the days ahead.

That evening Uncle Joseph set a few traps not far from their camp and explained to Benson how it was done. For supper they roasted yams over the open fire. Later, when Benson wearily stretched out on his sleeping mat, his mind wandered to his cousins. "I wonder what they learned at school today?" he mused. "I hope I can catch up with them when I get back to the farm. . . ."

In the distance he heard the weird, laughing cry of hyenas and the occasional snarl of a civet cat as he drifted off to sleep and the fire outside died down to glowing embers. It seemed he had barely closed his eyes when he heard Uncle Joseph calling, "Benson—time to get up!" The sky was only beginning to lighten in the east, but Uncle Joseph wanted to get an early start on setting traps.

Springing to his feet, the boy quickly stuffed some

kola nuts in the pockets of his ragged knickers and joined his uncle outside to begin the day's work. As he carefully observed everything the older man did, the young trainee quickly learned the routine of setting and unloading the traps. He also learned how to skin the animals and smoke the meat. He realized that though he was far from books, this too was education.

Every few days a worker came from the farm to collect the skins and meat and take them to market. But most of the time the two were alone in the bush. They spent their time setting traps, or at the camp skinning the day's catch and smoking the meat. At night they sat by the fire talking and eating the food Benson prepared—usually roasted rabbit or other small game.

Back at the farm, the boy had had little conversation with Uncle Joseph except to receive orders and discuss the farm work. But now, with no one else around to talk to, the older man seemed willing to treat his nephew more like a son. Despite his disappointment at being torn from his studies, Benson enjoyed the closeness with his uncle. It was almost like having a real father.

About two weeks into the trapping season, Uncle Joseph became ill and feverish. After a few days he broke out with the tell-tale spots and welts of chicken pox, and was too sick to work in the bush. Now the bulk of the work of setting and unloading the traps fell on Benson, and he had the extra burden of caring for his uncle as well. But despite their close living quarters and constant contact, Benson never contracted the disease. He would be forever grateful and mystified that he was somehow protected from it.

———

At the end of the three-month trapping season, Benson was glad to get back to the farm. He was especially hungry to borrow his cousins' books and try to catch up all the lessons he had missed. But the trapping expedition had gone well, and despite the lack of praise for his work, he knew it had been a profitable time for Uncle Joseph.

Months passed, and again it was year-end festival time at the Idahosa farm. Toiling extra hours to prepare for the holiday, Benson recalled painfully the incident with his uncle and the gift shirt from the year before. "Surely he'll give me the shirt this year," he reasoned. "I've learned to do my work better than before, and the trapping season went so well."

But Uncle Joseph quickly dashed any hopes the boy had. Claiming some chore had been overlooked, the unfeeling taskmaster once again withheld the coveted shirt from Benson while showering gifts upon his own children.

The unfairness was still far from over. Not just once, but two more times Uncle Joseph built up Benson's hopes of receiving the shirt. Each time there was an excuse not to give it. Benson never saw the shirt again, and had no doubt outgrown it anyway. But the pain of the experience left its mark for years to come.

# 4

# Home Again

It was now January, 1952, and Benson was a spindly fourteen-year-old. Tall and lean with work-hardened muscles, he carried an increasing load of duties on the farm while still trying to keep up with his cousins' studies. The dream of actually attending school never saw fulfillment during his three years of farming. But by this time, through persistent studying with his cousins, he could read fairly well and had mastered basic arithmetic.

One morning while spading the yam plots not far from the compound, Benson looked up to see two figures on bicycles approaching. "That's my father and older brother!" he exclaimed aloud, dropping his hoe. Instinctively he ran to meet them, heedless of the prospect of being scolded for leaving his work without permission. Reaching the compound just as the visitors dismounted their bicycles, he knelt and touched one knee to the ground. "Greetings, Father," he cried jubilantly. "You are welcome here!"

Just then Uncle Joseph came striding across the courtyard to greet his brother. "You are welcome, John," he said as the two men embraced.

John Idahosa turned toward Benson, taking note of

his tall body. "You are looking well, Son," he said with a smile. "Life on my brother's farm has been good to you."

Benson just nodded and grinned shyly, too nonplussed by his father's words of approval to know what to say.

After the traditional greetings and pleasantries had been exchanged, the two men sat down to talk and eat kola nuts, and the boys retreated a discreet distance. But Benson managed to overhear his father say the purpose of their visit was to take him home with them! His heart beat wildly in his chest when he thought of the prospect. He would see his mother again! And maybe— just maybe—he could persuade his father to let him go to school.

Out of a sense of duty he returned to his work in the yam plots, but for some reason the spading job seemed easier than before. That evening at supper it was confirmed: Benson would leave the next day with his father. The younger children moaned when they heard the news. They were losing their favorite storyteller and teacher!

After the meal he told them one last story, reviewed the day's lessons, then gathered his meager belongings for the journey home. His older brother shared his sleeping quarters that night, and Benson plied him with questions about his mother, his brothers and sisters, the village they were living in, and the school they attended. He found it hard to sleep with so many thoughts whirling in his head of what tomorrow held in store.

Early the next morning the two boys and their father set out on the journey with Benson riding on the rear fender of his brother's bicycle, his sparse baggage tied on his father's bicycle. Bumping over the rough road beneath a boiling sun, it was not exactly a pleasure excursion. His muscles became cramped from balancing his weight on the fender, and he constantly had to guard against catching his bare toes in the spokes when he rested his feet on the rear axle. But for Benson it was the trip of a lifetime. He was going home!

Just when he thought he was too weary to continue, his brother turned and said, "We're almost there!" Within a few minutes they approached a small group of mud houses and Benson saw his mother running toward them. He slid off the back of the bicycle even before it stopped and ran to meet her.

"Benson! Benson!" Sarah shouted with excitement, stretching out her arms toward him as he ran into her embrace. She hugged him close for a few moments, then held him at arm's length to look at this son who was now taller than she. "How you've grown!" she exclaimed, her eyes brimming with tears. "You went away a boy, but you've come home a young man!"

"It's good to be home, Mother," Benson said, his voice choked with emotion. "I've dreamed of this day for a long time."

Actually, "home" turned out to be a place he had never seen before. John Idahosa had moved his family to Uzea, the timber station where he was currently working. The nearest village was Uromi, twelve miles away, where the government school was located. Sarah had finally persuaded her husband to bring Benson home so he could enroll in school again. He was now able to work at about a fourth-grade level, but because he was considerably older than the other children in that grade, Sarah feared the headmaster might refuse to allow Benson to enroll. Her solution to the problem was to list his birthdate as September 11, 1941, though it was actually in 1939.

Benson almost shouted for joy when he learned he would be able to go to the local government school. For him it was no great hardship to trek the long distance each day. He preferred studying to any other activity— and it was infinitely more desirable than working on the farm. He applied himself to his studies and progressed rapidly in his classes during the two years he lived on that timber station. His greatest disappointment was that his father—always preoccupied with his work—remained aloof and exhibited little if any concern for his son. But Benson never gave up striving for acceptance and approval.

By the time he was sixteen years old, Benson's paternal grandmother in Benin City invited him to come live with her. For all practical purposes, she "adopted" him because of her feeling that the boy's father was not giving him proper attention. Also, she believed in reincarnation, and it was her conviction that Benson had actually been her grandfather in a prior existence, and for this reason she took a special interest in him. She agreed to pay his school fees at the Methodist boarding school about seventy miles away, and when school was not in session Benson lived with her and his grandfather.

In 1955 he was in Benin City during Christmas vacation when all the members of the Idahosa clan were gathered for the festivities. It was a special event because a favorite uncle, who worked as a customs officer and was usually stationed miles away on the Dahomey border, was home for the holidays.

As the feasting and merrymaking were drawing to a close, Benson suddenly realized that the next day he would have to take the bus back to his boarding school. The problem was he had no money for the bus fare. His grandmother was already stretching her limited resources to pay his school fees, which amounted to about $1.50 a month. He felt sure she would not be able to come up with the one shilling and sixpence he needed for the bus fare, and even if she could, he didn't want to ask her for it. She had assumed he would be able to earn his fare by selling newspapers and picking up other odd jobs. But the eager student had spent the vacation time catching up on his studies and doing extra reading in his textbooks. Now he was confronted with the ironic situation of having all his studies done, but being unable to get back to school for want of one-and-six (about eighteen cents)!

He slipped away from the crowd, sat down under a tree, and began to weep as the impossibility of the problem engulfed him. Just then his Uncle W.A.O. Bazuaye passed by and, seeing Benson's distress, stopped to ask what was wrong. When Benson told him the difficulty, the older man nodded sympathetically, then took out his change purse. "Here—I would like to help you," he said, handing Benson exactly one shilling and a sixpence piece. "Buy your bus ticket and go back to school."

---

Benson jumped to his feet and grabbed his uncle's hand. "Thank you, sir, thank you," he said excitedly. "I am so grateful for your help, and I hope someday I will be able to repay you."

"You can repay me by doing your best at school," Bazuaye replied, smiling and patting his nephew on the shoulder. "I am happy to see that you take your studies so seriously."

After completing his course at the boarding school, Benson returned to Benin City and lived with his grandmother. The only job he could find was selling newspapers on the street, and the pay was meager. He gave part of his earnings to his grandmother to help with food expenses, and he carefully saved enough money to buy his first pair of shoes.

He remembered the chagrin he had felt while living with Uncle Joseph when his cousins received gifts of splendid new clothes and shoes. All his life he had worn nothing but old, hand-me-down clothes. And he had always gone barefoot, which was not uncommon for Nigerian children. But it was a momentous day when at the age of eighteen he went into a shoe store and was fitted with a pair of size-nine men's shoes, paid for with his own hard-earned money. He bought a new shirt and trousers to go with them and for the first time in his life he felt truly prosperous.

At about this time his grandparents suggested that he move to another section of town, the Iyaro district, to live with his Aunt Beatrice, who operated a small hotel and restaurant there. She lived alone, and needed help with the business. Benson moved into her house, where he was grateful to have a quiet room all to himself. For his keep, he worked as houseboy helping with the cooking, cleaning and washing dishes in the restaurant.

He frequently visited his parents, who were now living at a timber station close to Benin City. Slowly, very slowly, it seemed John Idahosa's attitude toward his son was beginning to change. He occasionally asked for Benson's help with matters such as writing a letter or reading an important business document.

The young man's life style was quiet and exemplary. He tried to stay out of trouble, and he put forth every effort to improve himself. He seemed to be set apart from his family and peers. Yet something seemed to be lacking. His intuition told him that the Bini's centuries-long tradition of juju worship, sacrifice to idols, and belief in reincarnation proved no satisfactory answer to the riddle of life. Though his education was limited, he had already discovered that the more he learned, the more he was beset by insoluble questions. Where, then, was an answer to be found? And why did this questing spirit seem to smolder within him?

# 5

# A Bini Is Reborn

Sunday was always the most welcome day of Benson's week because it provided a diversion from the daily routine of working in the hot, crowded kitchen of the little hotel. After visiting the church services of various denominations in town, he had settled on the Salvation Army mission as his church. Some of his friends were members, and going to church held far more appeal for Benson than participating in his family's juju worship rites. So he joined the church choir and enjoyed the companionship of other young people his age. But the messages preached Sunday after Sunday failed to persuade him that becoming a Christian should be a life-changing experience.

After attending the morning service, Benson usually spent his Sunday afternoons playing soccer at a nearby schoolyard. He played the position of goalie, and had been chosen captain of his team.

One particular Sunday, Benson's team and another neighborhood team had just begun their game when they heard the sound of singing coming from a small church adjoining the playing field. The windows were open, and through a window just opposite one of the goals, they could see the back of the preacher's head.

The young men continued with their game, but they were distracted when the preacher began to speak and his sermon got louder and louder.

"I have an idea!" Benson shouted, motioning for the other players to gather around. "I'm going to kick this ball right through that window and hit the preacher in the head! I'll put a stop to all the noise that's disturbing our game."

"Great idea—go ahead!" they all encouraged him.

Benson skillfully dribbled the ball down the field with his feet, and when he got near the goal he kicked it high in the air toward the window. The ball hit the wall of the building and bounced back. He kicked again, and the ball hit the window frame and bounced back, while the preacher continued unperturbed.

"Try it again—you can do it!" some of his teammates shouted.

"I'll get him this time," Benson declared, the perspiration popping out on his forehead. He kicked again, harder than ever and at closer range. The ball again hit the window frame, but this time it bounced back and hit the young goalie square in the chest, throwing him to the ground.

"Benson, Benson!" his friend Bernard screamed, running over to kneel beside him. Benson lay stretched out on his back, the breath knocked out of him, too dazed to realize what had happened.

"Are you all right?" Bernard asked nervously, hovering over him. A few teammates gathered around, but most of them retreated a safe distance, fearful of being implicated in the incident.

Benson looked up to see a strange man standing over him with a concerned expression while Bernard explained what had happened. The stranger took charge of the situation. "Let's take him into the church," he said in a strong voice. Then it dawned on Benson—this was the preacher whom he had been trying to hit when the accident happened! Bernard and the preacher helped him to his feet and into the church, where he lay stretched out on a bench. His chest was now beginning to swell where the ball had hit him.

"We're going to pray for you in the name of Jesus and ask God to heal you!" the pastor declared.

Benson was amazed. Never in his life had he heard of anyone praying for healing in the name of Jesus. "I wonder if he knows I was trying to hit him with the soccer ball?" Benson questioned. "If he knew that, surely he wouldn't be praying for me to get well!"

The man laid his hand on Benson's chest and began to pray in a booming voice, the small congregation of about a dozen people joining with him. Benson suddenly felt a calmness come over him; he was able to get his breath, the swelling immediately began to go down, and his head stopped spinning. After a few minutes he sat up on the bench.

"I am Pastor Okpo," the man said, extending his hand. "You are welcome here; I believe Jesus has healed you."

"Thank you, sir," the young man replied, shaking his hand. "My name is Benson Idahosa."

Bernard, who had been waiting just outside the door, began calling, "Come on, Benson, we're waiting for you. Let's go back home."

Benson walked over to the doorway. "I want to stay and hear what this man has to say," he replied. "Why don't you come on in and stay with me?"

Bernard looked at him incredulously. "You can't stay here! You know these are Ibo people—and you are a Bini! They might try to kill you if you stay here by yourself."

"Bernard, this man just prayed and asked Jesus to heal me—why would he try to kill me? I believe I am healed, and I want to find out more about it."

"I'll wait for you out here," Bernard insisted, shaking his head. "You're not getting me into a meeting with a bunch of Ibos."

When Benson turned from the doorway, the small group of people had seated themselves again, and Pastor Okpo took up his sermon where he had left off. The young man sat down on the bench where he had been lying a few minutes before, and listened with rapt attention. What was so different about this preacher? He talked as if Jesus were his best friend who actually listened when he prayed. And his prayer had not been just a lot of flowery words—he prayed as if he expected things to happen, and they did!

At the close of the sermon, the pastor appealed for those who wanted to commit their lives to Jesus Christ and accept Him as Savior to come to the front of the church. Benson was the only one who responded. It was as if the entire meeting had been conducted for his benefit. He knelt on the dirt floor at the crude bench used for an altar and the pastor put his hands on

Benson's head and began to pray. Then he said, "Repeat after me the sinner's prayer."

Benson did not fully understand the significance of what he was doing, but he had felt drawn as if by a powerful magnet to that altar. While he repeated the sinner's prayer, a feeling of exhilaration welled up within him and he felt as if a great weight was lifted off his shoulders. "Jesus, I ask you to forgive my sins. . . . I accept you as Savior and Lord of my life. . . . I believe you are truly the Son of God, and I give my life to you."

When he got up from his knees, he felt like a brand-new person. Pastor Okpo shook his hand warmly and gave him a little red booklet. "This is a copy of a book from the Bible—the Gospel of John," he explained. "You should begin to read it every day; it will help you understand what it means to be a Christian. And on the back page are the words of the song you heard us sing today—'What a Friend We Have in Jesus.'"

As they started to leave, Benson explained he lived quite near the church, and invited the pastor to come to his house. They went out the door to find Bernard and a few faithful friends still waiting to be sure Benson got home safely. "You fellows go on," he told them. "I'm taking the pastor home with me for a visit."

The astonished soccer players watched in disbelief as their captain walked down the road talking happily with the man who a short time before had been the object of their scorn. Now Benson seemed to be hanging on every word the man said!

"I will knock on your door at five o'clock in the morning," Pastor Okpo said when they parted. "I want you to come with me to a prayer meeting at the church."

"I will be ready," the eager new convert responded. Benson told his aunt of his experience in the little church, but she showed no interest in her nephew's excitement over a tiny group of Ibo Christians. As far as the Binis were concerned, the Ibos were no better than slaves.

In his room alone that evening, Benson read the Gospel of John from cover to cover. This Jesus to whom he had committed his life that day seemed to come alive on the pages as he read. Long into the night he sang over and over, "What a Friend We Have in Jesus," too thrilled with his new experience to sleep more than a few hours.

At five o'clock he was up and dressed, waiting for Pastor Okpo to knock on his door. A bit surprised to see him at the prayer meeting, the small group of Ibo Christians welcomed their first Bini convert. Benson stayed at the church until seven-thirty that morning, praying with the others for the requests presented, and asking Pastor Okpo many questions.

"We will be having meetings here at the church on Wednesday and Thursday evenings," the pastor told him when it was time to leave. "You must come."

"I will be here," Benson promised.

He went about his tasks in the hotel kitchen with a new vigor that week. Any free time was taken with reading the Gospel of John, and he went back to the meetings to learn all he could from Pastor Okpo's sermons. Following the meeting on Thursday evening, the pastor took him aside for a moment. "Benson, you are the first Bini to accept Jesus in our little church, and we have been praying for your people for a long time," he said earnestly. "You must witness to your people about what God has done in your life, and urge them to come to church with you."

"Oh, I want to do that," Benson said, nodding vigorously. "I will talk to my friends on the soccer team, and to my neighbors."

"On Friday night we will have a study class to prepare for the Bible lesson on Sunday," the pastor said. "I hope you can come then, too."

"Yes, I will come," Benson agreed. "I want to learn all I can." At last he felt he was on the track of getting answers to the questions he had struggled with for so long.

On Saturday he spoke to a neighbor, Samuel, and asked him to go to Sunday school and church with him on Sunday. To Benson's delight, the man agreed. Pastor Okpo greeted them warmly when they arrived. "Benson, I would like you to teach the Sunday school lesson today," he said enthusiastically. "You can start a new class with your friend."

Fortunately, the conscientious young convert had written careful notes during the Friday night study session. So, using the notes, he taught his first Sunday school lesson to the lone pupil who had come with him. What he lacked in Bible knowledge, he made up for in enthusiasm. Samuel went forward and accepted Christ that afternoon in the main service, and agreed he would come back.

The next day, Benson met another friend, Michael Ajonuma, and related to him his experience of the prior week. "You must come and talk to my pastor," Benson insisted. "He can tell you what you must do to become a Christian, and pray for you."

They went to Pastor Okpo's house, only to find he was not at home. "Please come in," Mrs. Okpo invited when she learned the purpose of their visit. The pastor's wife answered Michael's questions, and at Benson's urging the young man knelt and committed his life to Christ. Now there were three converts from the proud Bini tribe.

During the following week Benson's friend Bernard came by the hotel to see him and found him out in the courtyard washing dishes. "We missed you at the soccer game last Sunday," he said, twirling a soccer ball in his hands. "We lost the game because we had to find another goalie. Can you come to practice with me when you finish your work?"

"I'm sorry, Bernard, but I have a church meeting to attend tonight," Benson answered. "Why don't you come with me to the meeting?"

Bernard shook his head in bewilderment. "I don't understand why you are so interested in that little Ibo church," he said. "If you're going to go to church, you could at least go to one of the larger, more respectable churches in town. What's wrong with the church you were attending before?"

"It's not just the church that is important," Benson explained as he stacked the clean bowls on a shelf just inside the door. "The important thing is that I have accepted Jesus Christ as my Savior, and He has completely changed my life."

"Well, you were already different from everyone else," Bernard argued. "That's why we nicknamed you 'Pastor'—because you never wanted to smoke and drink or chase girls with the rest of the guys. How is your life different now?"

"Bernard, those things just never interested me. And because my folks are so poor, I tried to behave myself so I wouldn't cause trouble for them. But since I've accepted Christ, I am changed on the *inside*—and that's far more important."

"But why does it have to be an Ibo church?"

"It doesn't matter that they are people of a different tribe," Benson countered as he picked up a broom and began sweeping the kitchen. "Pastor Okpo is a man of God, and I would rather hear him teach from the Bible than to play soccer. Since I am learning about God and His Son, Jesus, for the first time my life is beginning to make sense."

"It's okay for you, Benson," his friend said ruefully, tracing the seams of the soccer ball with his forefinger. "You've always been the religious type, anyway. But I can't see giving up soccer to go to a church meeting."

"I may still play soccer occasionally," Benson replied, stopping a moment to lean on the broom and gaze intently at his friend. "But serving the Lord and going to church are my most important activities, so I'm quitting the team. You'll have to get someone else to be goalie, and elect a new captain."

Over the next few weeks the eager convert shared his

new experience in Christ with everyone he saw—
relatives, neighbors and friends. It seemed all the Iyaro
district heard something dramatic had happened to
Benson Idahosa. It was as if a fire burned in his bones,
and nothing could deter him from witnessing to
everyone who crossed his path. Many of the young
people in the neighborhood laughed at him when he
preached on the street corner and passed out tracts. Yet
they were drawn to him because of his sincerity and
genuine interest in their welfare.

His family had always thought he was a bit strange
because he had no interest in juju worship, and had
always refused to eat food offered to the idols. Some of
the time he simply fasted on days when the food had
first been placed on the juju altar to placate the gods.
Later, when he moved in with his aunt, she prepared his
food separately, or he sometimes fixed meals for
himself.

"You'll get tired of this idea of being a Christian and
serving the white man's God," his relatives told him.
"You are a Bini, and some day you will return to the
gods of your ancestors."

But as the weeks went by, Benson's enthusiasm did
not wane. Rather, he became more and more zealous in
sharing his faith. In the meetings at the little Ibo
church, Pastor Okpo taught that after a believer's
conversion he should receive the Holy Spirit with the
evidence of speaking in other tongues, patterned after
the incident recorded in Acts 2:4.

"Jesus told his followers this gift of the Holy Spirit
would give them power to witness," he explained to his

young convert. Benson certainly wanted more power to witness to his friends and family, so he asked Pastor Okpo to pray with him that he would receive the Holy Spirit. Kneeling at the same altar where he had received salvation, as the pastor prayed Benson sensed the wind of the Holy Spirit sweeping over his being, and he began praising God in a language he had never learned. He had felt the presence of the Lord at the time of his conversion, but this sensation of feeling submerged in the presence of the Holy Spirit was more profound than anything he had yet experienced. It was a powerful reinforcement of his Christian faith.

He remembered an occasion several years before when his grandfather had explained to him that in the Edo language, the name Idahosa means "attentive to God." He knew that for his family, they took that to mean the god of their ancestors. But for Benson, it meant the God of the Bible who had so radically changed his life. And the young African wanted with all his heart to live up to his name by being attentive to God.

After becoming a Christian, Benson's thirst for knowledge was greater than it had ever been. While living with his aunt, he enrolled in a correspondence course from a private school in England, studying accounting and business administration. In exchange for serving as her houseboy and working in the hotel, his aunt provided him with a room, food to eat, and soap when he needed it, but no money for school fees or other luxuries. Unless he picked up an occasional odd job such as selling papers, he did not have so much as two shillings to jingle in his pocket.

Benson realized that unless he could get some education and therefore a paying job, he would be caught in the trap of poverty all his life. Now that he was a Christian, he wanted more than ever to break the pattern and improve himself. He worked hard on his correspondence course lessons, but one day a letter came saying unless he paid the tuition fees due immediately, he must drop the course. It was not the first such letter; he had enrolled in other such courses previously, only to be forced to drop out when the fateful letter of ultimatum arrived and he could not pay the fees. But this time he sought advice from his grandfather, chief of the Idahosa clan.

The older man was sympathetic to Benson's problem, and offered to help despite his grandson's strange religious interests. "I have a friend at the Bata Shoe Company who buys rubber from my rubber farm," the grandfather explained. "Come with me to see him, and I'll ask him to give you a job at the shoe company. Also, I'll give you a room here in my household so you can leave your aunt's place."

"If only your friend will give me the opportunity, I'll be a good worker," Benson promised his grandfather. "I don't want to be a houseboy for the rest of my life—"

"Don't worry—you are the brightest of all your father's sons," the older man said, smiling and patting his grandson on the shoulder. "You will make a good businessman. I'll see you first thing tomorrow morning."

Benson walked back to his aunt's house in a glow of excitement. Pastor Okpo had been teaching in the

Bible study that God is concerned about every area of the believer's life, and that He hears and answers prayer. "Thank you, Lord, that you promised to supply all our needs," Benson prayed that night before going to bed. "I trust you to provide a job for me. In Jesus' name, Amen."

# 6

# A Door of Opportunity

Benson was up earlier than usual the next morning to tend to chores for his aunt. He chopped firewood for cooking, filled the waterpots, and swept the house and the courtyard. Then he washed himself, using the last bit of soap his aunt had given him, and put on clean trousers and shirt and his only pair of shoes.

It took a full hour to walk from the Iyaro district to the forestry Road section of Benin City where his grandfather lived. But as he went the young man sang over and over, "What a friend we have in Jesus. . . ." He felt confident his new Friend would answer his prayer for a job.

He arrived at his grandfather's house, and the two of them walked the short distance to the offices of Bata Shoe Company. "What can I do for you today, Mr. Idahosa?" asked the manager when they stepped in the door of his office.

"I'd like you to meet my grandson Benson," the older man replied as they shook hands all around, then sat down. The two older men launched into conversation about the rubber business while Benson waited patiently and observed the activity in the outer office. It was his first opportunity to see firsthand the inner workings of such a business establishment. Finally his grandfather got around to the purpose of their visit—to ask about a job.

When the question was raised, the manager thoughtfully shifted the papers on his desk, then said, "Well, our stock clerk needs an assistant—I could let you try that job."

A surge of joy welled up within Benson when he realized his prayer was answered. He was sure all he needed was an opportunity to prove himself; determination and hard work would take over from there.

"Thank you, sir," Benson replied, smiling and getting to his feet.

"Report here for duty on Monday morning at 7:30," the office manager said, "and I'll take you to the stockroom."

The next day Benson moved his few belongings to his grandparents' house, where they provided him with a room that had a bed, a chair and a cupboard. To get to his room he had to walk right past the juju altar which dominated the main room of the house. Wanting to bear witness to his own Christian commitment, he painted a cross on one wall of his room and above it he lettered the slogan "God is with us." The next Sunday, while teaching a class at his church, he shared with the people how God had answered his prayer and provided a job.

From the first day at Bata Shoe Company, Benson quickly learned the procedures of his job and won the admiration of his superiors. When his first pay envelope came, he took out 20 percent of his earnings to give to the church and a small amount to buy soap. The rest he gave to his grandmother to save for him. Since he was making only about three dollars a week, it would take some time to build up any capital. But Benson's goal was to buy a piece of land, then build a house. Where education was concerned, he put all his efforts into studying the Bible with Pastor Okpo or reading any books and study aids he could get his hands on.

A few weeks after starting his job, he decided the time had come for a visit to his parents, who were now living in a village several miles from Benin City. Withdrawing most of his money from savings, Benson bought gifts of food and clothing for them, keeping back only enough for his round-trip fare by truck. Torn between feelings of excitement and anxiety, he set out on the journey.

While he bumped along for several hours in the back of the transport truck, he wondered how his father would respond to this visit.

Over the years his attitude toward Benson had softened somewhat, but many months had passed since they had seen each other. "I hope Father will approve of me now that I have a job," he mused, "and I hope he likes the gifts I got for him. . . ."

At the Idahosa compound, the young man found only his mother at home while the younger children were at school.

"Benson!" Sarah cried, running across the courtyard to meet him. "I'm so glad to see you!" Mother and son embraced, then he sat down to rest in the shade while she brought him a gourd cup of cool water. "We heard the news that you had moved to your grandfather's house and that you have a job now," Sarah said, her face beaming. "The gods are good to you."

Benson smiled at her, shaking his head. "The gods had nothing to do with it, Mother," he said. "I have found the only true and living God, and He has answered my prayers. That's why I'm here—to tell you what has happened to me, and to bring gifts to you and to Father."

He opened the bundle beside him and took out several large yams and a sack of rice and presented them to her.

"Thank you, Son," Sarah responded. "You are kind to bring such gifts. John will be home soon and will be happy to see you. But what is this about the only true and living God? We believe in juju and make sacrifices to the gods of our ancestors, as Binis always have done."

"You know I have never believed in juju, Mother. I've always thought it was dirty, and I wanted nothing to do with it. But now I have found the truth, and for the first time in my life I have peace in my heart." Benson's face glowed with fervor as he went on to share the full story of his conversion, and Sarah listened in rapt attention.

"I want you to find the same peace in knowing Christ that I have found," Benson said, gripping her hand. "I want you to burn your juju idols and accept Jesus as your Lord and Savior."

Sarah sat staring at the ground, trying to take in all she had heard. "If I burn the idols, the gods will be angry and might put a curse on us," she said, searching his face, trying to understand this son who had always seemed to be so different from the other children.

"Believe me, Mother, those gods can do nothing for you. They are only dead sticks of wood. Your only hope for salvation is to put your trust in Jesus Christ, the Son of God."

The air was heavy with silence for several moments. "I will think about it, Benson," Sarah finally responded. "I can see that something wonderful has happened to you, and I would like to have the peace you are talking about. But I will wait and see what your father says."

She got up and headed for the cooking shed. "It's time I got the cooking pot on—I bought things at market this morning to fix okra stew."

"I'll chop more firewood for you," Benson said, getting to his feet. "I'm not a houseboy anymore, but I haven't forgotten how to chop wood!"

Early in the evening when John Idahosa returned home from his timber station, he was surprised to find his son Benson sitting on the ground in the courtyard talking intently with the younger children crowded around, hanging on every word he said. The pungent smell of okra stew filled the air.

When Benson saw his father, he jumped to his feet and ran to greet him, clasping his hand and touching one knee to the ground. The hard lines of John's face softened a bit as he shook his son's hand and said, "You are welcome here."

Sarah bustled across the courtyard to greet her husband. "The stew will soon be ready," she said. "Shall I serve you and Benson in your quarters?"

"Yes," John answered. "I want to hear all about

Benson's job—we have many things to talk about." He walked toward his room, motioning for his son to come along. Benson picked up his bundle from the ground nearby and followed, praying for guidance as he went.

I brought these gifts for you, Father," Benson said once they were within the privacy of John's room. "I want you to know I appreciate all you have done for me, and I am proud to be your son."

John opened the bundle of clothing, obviously touched by such a splendid gift, though his face showed little emotion. "Thank you, Son," he said softly, fingering the fine embroidery on one of the shirts. "I appreciate your presents."

"I bring you greetings from your father and mother and your people in Benin," Benson said. "They all wish you well."

Sarah brought bowls of rice and stew, and the two continued to visit and exchange news as they ate. After finishing the last grain of rice, Benson at last broached the subject that had been burning in his bones. "Father, one of the main reasons I've come to visit is to tell you that my life has been totally changed in the past few months since I have accepted Jesus Christ."

John looked at his son quizzically, but kept on eating and nodded for Benson to continue.

The young man shared the full story of his experience, praying silently that the truth of Jesus Christ would pierce his father's heart. A holy boldness seemed to possess him as he declared, "Father, I want you to burn your juju idols and accept Jesus Christ as your Lord and Savior. That is the only way you can find peace with God."

A look of vexation crossed the older man's face and he shook his head. "But these are gods of our ancestors," he said, motioning toward the idols and the juju altar in the room. "We must pray to them to protect us. I am the prince of juju for the Idahosa clan, and I must fulfill my responsibility to assure the safety of my people. I am glad if you have found peace in Jesus Christ, but the thing you are asking me to do is impossible."

"Father, those idols have no power to protect you from evil spirits—it is Jesus who has the power to protect you, not the spirits of your ancestors. If you put your faith in Jesus, no evil spirit can touch you!"

John Idahosa looked with wonder at this young man before him whose eyes burned with the zeal of his message and who spoke with such authority. Could this be the son he had told Sarah to throw on the garbage heap more than twenty years ago? Could it be that the child he had considered the most worthless of all his offspring was actually the most gifted? If only he were not obsessed with these strange ideas about some man called Jesus Christ.

The older man stood up, indicating the discussion was over. "I will consider what you have said," he promised, extending his hand. "Thank you for your visit; I hope you will come again."

Benson was instantly on his feet, clasping his father's hand in both his own. "Thank you, Father—I will be praying every day that you will accept the truth of Jesus Christ."

Back in Benin City, Benson went about his work at

the shoe company with great diligence. But the desire to share the message of Jesus Christ with his people became a compelling drive. He frequently visited the Iyaro district where he had lived with his aunt and witnessed to his friends. With Pastor Okpo's encouragement, he began organizing teams of workers and going out into the villages surrounding Benin City to preach the gospel that had so radically changed his own life. Wherever he went with his burning message, people seemed drawn to him as a moth is drawn to a flame.

# 7

# The Vision

Because he was from the Benin tribe, Benson had access to villages the Ibo Christians had been unable to reach. He would take a team to a village and make a call on the chief to obtain his permission to preach to the people. The group would begin singing gospel choruses, and soon a crowd would gather.

The people seemed open to his message. They were especially amazed when Benson preached on healing and then prayed for the sick—and they began seeing miracles of healing take place before their eyes.

In the village of Nifor, a woman who had suffered epileptic seizures was instantly healed. As the word spread, many more sick people came to the meetings and found healing—one man was healed of cancer, another of whooping cough. There were almost as many maladies as there were people. Scores of villagers accepted Christ as Savior as they saw evidence of His power. Within a short time preaching and teaching in the villages became such an all-consuming weekend activity that Benson found it difficult to get back to Benin City to his job on Monday mornings.

Because of the distances and rigors of travel over the dirt roads and trails through the bush, he finally went to his superiors with a request: Could he have permission to work five days a week instead of six, to allow for travel time in getting to and from the villages? The directors at Bata were greatly impressed by Benson's scrupulous performance on the job, as well as by his positive effect on the morale of his fellow-workers. They granted his request without hesitation, so Benson's evangelistic activities increased even more.

By this time he had received a salary increase and his future in the business world looked good. But the young preacher looked on his job as simply a means of making a living and helping him to assist his family and some of the needy pastors with whom he worked.

Two years after beginning his job with Bata Shoe Company, Benson was promoted to assistant stock keeper and given another salary increase. He was now twenty-five years old, and he felt the time had come for him to live independent from his grandparents. He rented a small apartment in the Forestry Road section of town, and his grandmother gave him the furniture from his room to set up housekeeping in the new location. At about the same time, he withdrew most of his savings to buy a plot of ground on which he planned some day to build a house.

The driving force in his life was a burning desire to preach the message of salvation and to lead people to decide for Christ. But despite the fact impressive numbers were becoming Christians, Benson carried a special burden for his own parents' salvation. By now he had visited them on numerous occasions and repeatedly urged them to renounce juju worship and accept Jesus, but their fear seemed to hold them back.

John Idahosa had gradually come to respect Benson, and even sought his help and advice on business matters occasionally. He was proud of his son the preacher, but the bonds of tradition kept him from accepting such a revolutionary message as the Christian gospel.

On one such visit to the Idahosa compound, Benson found that his father was gone on a business trip, and his mother was failing in health from a stomach disorder. He determined not to leave her until he was assured of her salvation. Upon her son's insistence, Sarah gathered her juju idols and fetishes and burned them, then knelt and repeated after him a prayer of commitment to this Jesus she had heard so much about. At last she understood what Benson meant when he said a profound peace had engulfed him.

"Now I feel what you feel," she said with delight, getting up from her knees and hugging him. "In juju worship, all I knew was fear—but Jesus brings joy and peace."

Benson instructed her in prayer and witnessing, and directed her to a nearby full-gospel church where she could meet other Christians. After a final prayer with her, he made the return journey to Benin City, but this time with the joy of knowing he had raided the enemy's territory and been victorious.

When John learned of Sarah's decision he did not object, but for himself he was still reluctant to forfeit his rank as prince of juju for the Idahosa clan.

Several months later Benson was surprised by a visit

from one of his cousins who lived in Ewasso, the village of Sarah's people. The cousin brought sad news: Sarah was dead. Her ailment had worsened, and she had gone to Ewasso to stay with her family so they could care for her. "Her dying request was that she didn't want juju burial rites," the cousin reported. "We've come to ask you to take charge of the arrangements."

Benson got leave from his job and took some friends from his church with him on the journey to Ewasso. He conducted a Christian burial for his beloved mother, and once again took advantage of the opportunity to witness to his father.

"I think your message is right, Son," John told him. "And I'm glad Sarah became a Christian. But I must consider it further. . . ."

Benson returned home with a heavy heart, haunted by the look of emptiness on his father's face. "Oh, God," he cried, "I pray he will accept Jesus as Savior before it's too late. . . ."

Three more years rolled by, during which Benson applied himself to preaching and witnessing with greater and greater fervor. He bought his first motorcycle and was then able to reach still more villages with the gospel. At his job he was promoted to the finance department and given another salary increase, plus extra commissions based on shoe sales. But climbing the corporate ladder had no allure for him; the higher calling to share his faith in Jesus claimed top priority.

Then came the tragedy of civil war. In June, 1967, leaders of the Eastern Region of Nigeria, in protest against the existing military government, declared their region to be an independent republic called Biafra. Death and destruction spread across southeastern Nigeria as conflict between government and revolutionary forces continued for almost three years, often claiming innocent victims caught in the crossfire.

One such victim was John Idahosa. After Sarah's death he had reestablished contact with his second wife, who had gone to live with her family near the Biafran border. She had agreed that on a certain date she would come visit John at the village where he was currently working. When she did not appear on the appointed day, John decided to go to her family's village in search of her. He advised a few friends where he was going and set out on the journey.

Several days passed and John did not return, so the concerned friends went to find him. On the way they passed through an area where Nigerian troops and Biafran revolutionaries were fighting. They spotted a Biafran Landrover with prisoners of war sitting in the back under armed guard. Among those captured was John Idahosa. The friends went to John's wife and reported what they had seen, and she in turn traveled to Benin City to take the news to Benson's older brother.

When Benson looked up one day to see his brother standing at the door of his apartment, he knew some important news must be forthcoming. The brothers rarely saw one another, especially since John—their father's namesake—had been serving as a sergeant in the Nigerian army.

"I've asked for and received a leave from duty," John said after relating the news of their father's capture.

"I'm taking a party of soldiers to the area where he was last seen to conduct a search. Maybe we can find him."

"May God go with you," Benson responded. "I pray you will succeed."

But the mission proved fruitless. In spite of a thorough search and investigation, the party found no evidence that the elder John Idahosa was still alive. He was assumed dead, and according to custom, the younger John took on the responsibilities as chief elder of the Idahosa family.

"If only I had pressed him to make a decision for Christ," Benson agonized when the report came back. "I hope he realized before it was too late that his juju gods could not protect him, and called upon the Lord for salvation. . . . At least I had told him how to accept Jesus Christ as his Savior."

He relived the occasion of his last visit to his father's house near a remote timber station about a year earlier. A friend had lent him a car to make the trip, and Benson and his father had greatly enjoyed being together.

"I know you're right," the older man had said, nodding his head in agreement when Benson urged him to confess Christ. "Some day I expect to become a Christian—but not right now. Later. . . ."

And so Benson had returned to Benin City, not realizing he would never see his father alive again. For weeks and months the uncertainty of his father's fate weighed on Benson's heart, but he knew he had had his last opportunity to witness to John Idahosa.

"Lord," he prayed, "I realize more than ever before

that a person's salvation must not be taken lightly. From this day on, whenever I share the gospel with someone, I will press that person for a decision." The experience served only to fuel the fire that already burned in his bones.

One night, about a year after his father's disappearance, Benson was abruptly awakened from sleep by the sound of a voice speaking to him. He sat up in bed, instantly alert. He knew it was a message from the Lord himself.

*"I have called you that you might take the gospel around the world in my name,"* the voice said in a strong, assuring tone. *"Preach the gospel, and I will confirm my Word with signs following."*

The room seemed charged with the presence of God as Benson fell to his knees beside the bed. "Lord, wherever you say to go, I will go," he pledged. "Whatever you say do, I am going to do." He prayed on through the night, renewing his own vows to God and interceding for his people who were yet to hear the message of salvation.

The following night, he was again awakened quite suddenly. This time he felt himself leaving the room, traveling effortlessly through the air for some distance, until he came to a huge field. The plot was empty except for a great tree standing in the middle, but the tree was completely dead from its roots to its topmost branch. Benson was aware that the Lord was beside him, though he saw no figure.

*"Stand under the tree,"* the Lord instructed. *"Someone will come and ask you for help."*

Benson stood obediently. He looked up to see an old woman who appeared to be in her eighties walking slowly toward him. She was stooped over, carrying a heavy load on her head. *"Go near and help her,"* the Lord said.

Benson moved to her side. "Mama, could I help you with your load?" he asked, taking her arm.

The old woman peered up at the straight young man standing before her. "I have passed so many on the road," she said in a cracked, weary voice, "and no one helped me."

Benson helped her take the load down, then guided her to stand under the tree. Suddenly a breeze began blowing, and looking up, Benson saw that a bright green leaf had sprouted at the top of the tree. Looking off to the distance, he saw two elderly men approaching, carrying heavy loads on their heads. "Can I help you?" he called to the men.

"Yes," they answered. "We have been looking for someone to help us drop our loads."

He eased their loads to the ground, and the men stood beside the old woman under the tree. Again looking up at the branches, Benson saw that two more fresh, new leaves had sprouted.

More and more people started coming toward him. At the far edge of the field, Benson noticed there was a two-lane road. One lane led directly to the spot where he was standing; the other curved and led off away from the field. A few people were walking in the lane leading into the distance, but most of them were on the road headed straight toward the tree. They all carried heavy loads.

---

As they approached, Benson worked feverishly helping people put down their loads. Soon about a hundred people were standing under the tree, relieved of their burdens. By this time, Benson was becoming very tired. Again the voice spoke to him.

*"Look and see that among those you have helped are some with more stamina than you now have. Ask them to join you in helping the multitudes who are still coming."*

Benson turned to the crowd. "Young men," he called, "I am almost exhausted. Why don't you join me in helping to take down the loads of these weak ones who are coming?"

Several strong young men came forward, and together they helped remove the loads of the passersby who came by the tree. The vision continued for almost an hour, and during that time the entire field was filled with a great multitude of people. Each one received help to unload his or her heavy burdens as more and more young men joined Benson in the work.

Looking up at the tree, Benson was startled to see the branches densely covered with leaves. Not only had foliage appeared, but the branches had spread out to cover the entire field and provide shade for all those who stood beneath. The tree which had once been dead was now vibrant with life.

The voice spoke again. *"This is what I shall do with your life. If you will begin to help people drop their burdens at my feet, I will bring back to life that which was dead. Just as you are now standing before this great multitude, you will one day stand before thousands*

*around the world and speak of my great power to heal
and perform miracles."*

Seeing that life had come again to the tree, and that
the people had been set free from their burdens, Benson
began to sing:

Come to Jesus, Come to Jesus, Come to Jesus
now. . . . He will save you, He will save you, He
will save you now.

The crowd joined him in the refrain, and they all
began singing and rejoicing before the Lord as Benson
led them. Looking around, he saw that the old ones
who had been weak and stooped over were now
standing straight. The more they sang and rejoiced, the
stronger they became, for the power of the Lord was
present to heal and strengthen.

Suddenly Benson felt himself again being transported,
and he was back in his room. The vision was over.

In the days following, he began seeing a greater
response to his ministry as he traveled from village to
village. Instead of groups of a dozen or fifteen people,
the crowds numbered from thirty-five to a hundred,
and sometimes more. When he would call on a chief to
ask permission to preach in a village, he found a more
willing response than he had seen before. He seemed to
preach with greater power. More people confessed
Christ as their Savior, and more healings occurred as
he prayed for the sick.

In areas where a full-gospel church was already
established, Benson referred converts from his meetings

to that church and urged them to become faithful in attending. But many villages had no such church within walking distance. In these cases, Benson and his co-workers would try to visit as often as possible to instruct the converts in their new-found faith. Pastor Okpo provided guidance and direction for his zealous young convert, and encouraged him in every way.

The section of Benin City where Benson was now living had no full-gospel church, and he felt the need to begin instructing the new Christians in the area in their walk with the Lord. He began searching for a location, and found a small storefront building on Forestry Road that could be rented for twelve dollars a month. After paying the first month's rent with his own money, he began spreading the word in the neighborhood that Bible studies would be offered there several nights a week.

Benson's own knowledge of the Bible had come primarily through what he had learned from Pastor Okpo, from a few seminars he had been able to attend, and from correspondence courses he had obtained from England and America. But he instinctively knew that if the new converts were going to grow into strong, effective Christians, they must learn the Word of God. As he began teaching the small group which showed up at the beginning, interest grew quickly and the attendance increased.

Though he continued his job at the shoe company, Benson realized his greatest responsibility was to evangelize and to teach the small group of new converts coming each week to the storefront building. He was now thirty years old, and he began to feel he should find a helpmeet to work with him in the ministry. As in every other important decision of his life, he prayed earnestly for the Lord's guidance in the matter of a wife.

# 8

# The Pastor Takes a Wife

A few months after Benson's conversion, a friend in the Iyaro district had introduced him to a special young lady, Margaret Izevbigie, while she was home from boarding school for the holidays. He took a special interest in her, perhaps because she was an only child whose parents were separated. She was living with her mother, who was a princess of juju, which meant idol worship was a way of life in their household.

Benson shared the gospel with Margaret, just as he had with everyone else in that part of town, but she joined in with her friends who made fun of his preaching, calling him "Little Pastor." Yet she couldn't help liking him; he seemed so friendly and concerned about her. They both came from the Benin tribe, and spoke the Edo language.

"You need a brother or someone to protect you in this wicked neighborhood," Benson told the attractive young girl one day. "Let me be your older brother to give you advice and look after you." She agreed, not realizing how profoundly that accord would affect her future. Benson remembered his own loneliness without the influence of his father, and he hoped to spare her that pain.

Soon the word went out in the Iyaro district. "You'd better not bother Margaret. If 'the pastor' hears about it, you'll be in trouble. He doesn't want anyone picking on her." And the "pastor" laid out some rather strict rules he wanted his young charge to follow. The rules included such things as not going to a dance with any boy, and not following any boy to the community water tap unless Benson was also there.

"If you find a young man who wants to marry you, bring him to me and I will tell you if he is okay for you," he instructed her.

Margaret, who was fifteen years old when she met Benson, followed his rules, and everyone regarded her as his little sister. Yet for several years she did not respond to the gospel message he continued to share with her and her mother and other relatives. But during this time she brought several prospective suitors to him for approval. He rejected every one of them, and she accepted his judgment.

One afternoon when Benson and one of his converts stopped at Margaret's house for a visit, they found the place full of her relatives. Everyone seemed quite agitated, and many of the women were crying. "What's going on?" the young man inquired.

"It's my uncle's baby," Margaret explained, wiping her tears with the back of her hand. "She has been sick for several days, and this morning she died. She kept having convulsions, but nothing the local doctors could do helped her. We even made sacrifices at the juju shrine here in our house, but she died anyway."

"Where is the baby now?" Benson asked.

---

"There," Margaret answered, gesturing toward the bedroom. "We've already bathed the body and bought the coffin for her burial."

Benson felt a righteous indignation burning within him. He turned to the father of the baby. "The God I serve can bring your baby back to life," he said confidently. "Will you permit me to pray for her?" Startled, the father agreed, though he himself was not a Christian, nor were any of the other family members.

Benson walked boldly into the next room where the cold, still form of the baby lay on the bed. He ordered everyone out except his Christian companion, and closed the door. The relatives waited obediently in the other room, weeping and mourning. Benson's voice boomed with authority as he and his co-worker prayed earnestly for the baby to be restored to life. Several minutes passed.

Suddenly the startled relatives heard the baby sneeze. They rushed into the room to find she was awake and looking perfectly normal. "She is going to be all right," Benson told the mother, who gathered the child in her arms. "Fix her something to eat."

Margaret was deeply moved by the event. She felt shame for the times she had laughed at the young preacher and had thrown away the gospel tracts he had given her. He had repeatedly told her and her friends that this Jesus to whom he prayed was a God of power. "Maybe there is something to what he's preaching, after all," she thought. "His God has done something truly wonderful." That night, in the solitude of her room, she asked Jesus to forgive her sins and come into her life.

---

The next morning Benson came by again. He found the baby quite well, and Margaret told him of her decision. "There is a meeting tonight at the church in the school compound not far from here," he told her. "You should try to come."

"I will be there," she promised, somewhat to his surprise.

That night she joined in the singing and praying with the small congregation. When the pastor preached on the Second Coming of Christ, she rejoiced that she was now prepared to meet Him. Over the following days Benson explained to Margaret the errors of juju worship. Not only did she totally renounce it; she began witnessing to her mother.

"Mother, faith in Jesus Christ can do more for you than worshiping juju idols," the daughter told her. "'Those idols did nothing for your brother's dead baby." But the grip was too strong. The older woman had built a shrine to Olokun, the god of water, and set aside two rooms in her house for juju worship. She was not prepared to give it all up on the strength of one miracle.

Several months had passed, and Margaret was back home in the Iyaro district after completing her course of study at the teachers' training college. Benson came to visit her one evening in quite a serious mood. They sat in the courtyard behind the house to talk. He was straightforward about what was on his mind.

"Margaret, I've been praying about finding a wife," he said. "I believe the Lord has shown me that you are the one I am to marry."

The young woman, taken completely by surprise, began to weep. "You have known me all these years, and you have treated me as if you were my brother," she said. "I suppose you've been planning this all along—why didn't you say something to me? How can I marry you if you're my brother!"

"Please believe me, Margaret," he protested. "I've not been planning this at all; I have really thought of you as a younger sister. Only recently while praying about a wife has the Lord shown this to me. But I do believe I have heard from God."

The distraught young woman, usually quite composed, continued weeping, and Benson decided to go talk to her mother. "I want to marry your daughter," he said, and then went on to explain why Margaret was weeping.

He became a bit rattled when the mother also began to weep! But soon he realized she was weeping for joy. "I will be so grateful to have you for a son!" she exclaimed. Though she still practiced juju worship, she had no objection to her daughter marrying a Christian.

But in the ensuing days Margaret, quite shy and reserved by nature, raised another objection. "I don't want to be the wife of a pastor," she told him, shaking her head emphatically. "You teach a Bible study and lead the youth group and that is quite enough. But a pastor is so open to criticism from everyone in the church—your life is not your own. I don't want any part of that."

"Don't worry about whether I am a pastor or not," he insisted. "What you must do is give your life more fully to the Lord, and ask Him what your part in the ministry should be."

She had a ready answer for that. "My part in the ministry is to go to church and worship God, then go home. But to marry a *pastor*—that would be too much!"

In the end, Benson's charm and persuasion won the day. He still held a good position at Bata Shoe Company, thus technically he was not a full-time pastor—just a businessman who happened to do a lot of witnessing on the side. So with the help of a woman in the church who knew how to handle all the details, wedding preparations began. On April 6, 1969, the two were married in the little storefront building where Benson had been teaching Bible studies. Margaret took on the responsibility as woman of the house in Benson's small apartment, and she also began teaching in a nearby primary school.

The marriage was only a few weeks old when some of Margaret's fears began to be realized. Her idea of a quiet, orderly life with the husband she loved remained only a dream. Benson continued his practice of going straight from his job to the little church for Bible study several times a week. She never knew for sure when or if he would be home for meals. Spending time at home with his bride seemed to be at the bottom of his list of priorities, while it was at the top of hers.

She became a "weekend widow" as Benson gathered teams of young people together and went off preaching in the villages and in secondary boarding schools of the surrounding area.

"Benson, I may as well not even have a husband," she complained to him. "I hardly ever see you—we never have any time together alone. You see, this is one of the reasons I didn't want to marry a pastor."

"But, Margaret, you need to become involved in what I'm doing," he would coax. "If you realized how desperately these people need the gospel, you would want to reach out to them." Then he related to her the vision God had given him a few years before, and how he felt God had placed a special call on his life. "I want to see that dead tree come to life," he said with zeal burning in his eyes. "And I want you to be a part of what God is going to do."

The young couple began praying and reading the Bible together, and finally Margaret agreed to go with the group on a witnessing trip to the village of Etete, about four miles from Benin City. Arriving in the early evening, the young people scattered in every direction and delivered a gospel tract to each house in the village. Then they gathered in a central place and began singing gospel choruses.

One by one the children and young people in the village began to gather, and finally several adults stood at the back of the crowd to listen as Benson preached. By the time the gospel team headed back to Benin City, a number of people had come to the Lord and some had been healed as Benson prayed for them. When the team visited the village a week later to conduct a prayer meeting, several of the new converts attended and testified of their new-found faith in Christ.

Margaret found that the more she went out on the

witnessing trips, the greater joy she felt, and the more interested she was in the spiritual needs of the people. Also, it was a way she and Benson could have more time together and more common experiences to share.

Her resentment of the ministry gradually disappeared, but one problem remained. She had always believed that "the way to a man's heart is through his stomach." But she soon realized that this husband of hers had no interest in food whatsoever.

Benson's custom was to leave the apartment at about five-thirty in the morning to go to the church prayer meeting, then return for breakfast about seven o'clock. But breakfast usually consisted of little more than a cup of tea. Then he would be off to his job, and Margaret went to teach her classes at the primary school. In the afternoon she would return to do household chores and prepare their evening meal. Sometimes he would come to eat; sometimes not. And all too often he would arrive home and announce, "I don't feel like eating tonight." Then he would prepare to go to a meeting at the church, and his new bride would sit at the table and cry.

"Look, why don't you tell me what kind of food you like, so I'll know what to prepare," Margaret told him one evening. "You are much too thin—you have to eat. I would like people to see a difference in you now that we are married!" And the tears flowed copiously.

"I'm sorry, Margaret," Benson replied, trying to comfort her. "There is nothing wrong with the meals you prepare—it's just that I'm not all that interested in food. The work of the Lord is so much more important."

The young bride began praying earnestly for God to

show her what to do about her husband's food. And gradually Benson adjusted to having regular meals and eating the chicken or rice or vegetables his wife put before him. He even began gaining a few pounds.

About four months after the wedding, Margaret attended a camp meeting in Benin City conducted by an interdenominational evangelical group. The series of Bible study sessions challenged her in a new way to commit her life totally to Christ, and to witness boldly about her faith to others. She had a new hunger to learn all she could about the Bible, and what had once seemed confusing began to make sense to her. It was a spiritual turning point for the young preacher's wife, who had had such problems accepting the idea of being in the ministry.

But it seemed that just as one problem was resolved, another difficulty loomed on the horizon—one the young couple had not counted on. A year went by, and Margaret did not conceive. Her family anxiously awaited word that a baby was on the way, but the word did not come. Margaret's mother was especially eager to have a grandchild by her only child.

Meanwhile, Benson's family became angry because he had married a woman without testing her beforehand to be sure she was able to bear children. This is a common custom in Nigeria, because to the African it is supremely important to have children. Benson had refused to abide by the custom, following instead the Christian resolve of chastity before marriage. He was convinced Margaret was God's choice for his wife, and he believed God would honor their union with children.

---

"Don't worry," he assured his bride. "God has promised me that you will bear children. We must keep our faith in Him, and He will work in His own time."

But as month after month went by, Margaret sometimes wondered if perhaps God had forgotten her.

# 9

# Opposition From Within

People were crowding into the little storefront building on Forestry Road for Bible study sessions, and often spilling into the walkway and the street. They seemed to have an insatiable appetite to learn more about this strange new book and its gripping message. Benson worked at his job at Bata Shoe Company in the daytime, taught the Bible study sessions in the evening, and usually traveled to the surrounding villages to preach on weekends. He was too busy to worry about solving the problem of overcrowding in the storefront.

After conducting meetings in the rented building for several months, Benson had a dream that was to affect the scope of his ministry radically. In his dream he saw a short street leading off a main road in the Iyaro district of Benin City, behind the University of Benin. Trooping out of this street toward the main road was a large crowd of people. They seemed to be happy people.

He awoke abruptly. "What have I seen?" he questioned.

He lay down again, puzzling over what the dream meant, when the Lord spoke to him: *"In that place is some vacant land I have kept for myself to begin a work for my glory."*

Benson could scarcely wait until morning to ride his motorcycle to Iyaro and find the landlord who owned that piece of property. He found the man and told him, "The Lord spoke to me last night about some land behind the university. I saw a crowd of people coming out to the main road, and the Lord told me He has kept a piece of land vacant there to be used for His glory."

Surprisingly, the owner responded by quoting the Bible. " 'The earth is the Lord's, and the fullness thereof,' " he said (Ps. 24:1). "I have no land of my own—but I wish I did, because I would give it to you. The only land on that street is a fifty-by-one-hundred-foot lot, and I consider that this belongs to my second son. It is already written in my will. If you want to talk to him and give him money to buy land in another location, I will ask him to release it to you."

"Your son is my dear friend," Benson answered. "I'm going to tell him what God has shown me. I'll be back to see you this evening."

Benson mounted the motorcycle again, and weaving through the noisy city traffic, made his way to the school where his friend was teaching. He waited outside the door until the lecture was finished, then walked into the classroom and greeted the rather startled teacher.

"I've just come from a visit with your father," Benson began. "He told me there is a small piece of land behind the university that he has allocated to you in his will. I have come to explain to you how God showed me that land belongs to Him and we are to use it for a church."

The young man sat on the corner of his desk, threw his head back and laughed uproariously. "How can

God take my land from me and give it to the church?" he asked. "What kind of God is that?"

"Well, the Lord needs it," Benson explained. "We are going to give you money to go and buy a bigger piece of land."

The man smirked, shaking his head. "You won't be able to give me enough money."

"How much money do you ask?"

"Four hundred pounds," he answered—which was about six hundred dollars, an enormous amount of money for a little prayer group whose income at the time was sixteen dollars a month, of which twelve went to pay rent on the store building.

"How many years will it take you to get four hundred pounds?" the teacher asked with a derisive grin.

"Less than one month," Benson answered confidently.

The young man looked at him in disbelief, then said, "Okay—if you bring me the money you can have the land."

"It's a deal," said Benson, extending his hand. The teacher stood up, gave a rather uncertain handshake, and Benson strode out the door. He went on to his duties at his job that day, but as he worked he mentally rehearsed how he would present the project to the Bible study group.

That evening when the people crowded into the tiny building, Benson shared his vision about the piece of land, and his visit to the teacher that day. "The Lord told me to hurry up and the land would be provided for us," he reported. They voiced their agreement, then cheers and shouts filled the room as the enthusiastic worshipers praised the Lord together.

The next morning, a Thursday, Benson went again to see the landowner.

"My people agree that we should have this land to build a church," Benson told him. "On Sunday we will ask everyone in the group to give money to buy the land from you."

Still dubious, the man asked, "How many people are in your congregation?"

"I expect we'll have about forty on Sunday," Benson answered.

"You'll never make it," the landowner said, shaking his head. "Even the largest cathedral in town can barely manage to collect one hundred pounds—how can you hope to get together the price I've asked in less than one month, with only forty people?"

"You'll see," Benson said, flashing a broad smile. "God has promised us this land, and He will provide."

On a Sunday in April, 1970, for the first time in his life, Benson asked the people to give offerings and make pledges toward the amount needed to buy the land. The response produced even more than he had asked for. From the group of about forty people, six hundred and eighty dollars was given or pledged, and those who pledged said they would pay within one month.

"If we could borrow the money, we could get the land even more quickly," the young pastor reasoned. "Then we could pay back the loan when the pledges come in."

He immediately began to call on some of his relatives and shared with them how the people were giving from their meager incomes in order to buy land for a church. A number of the relatives, though they themselves were not Christians, were impressed by Benson's enthusiasm and the dedication of his people, and they made cash loans toward the project. Some of the people who had made pledges managed to borrow money to pay the pledges at once. By the end of that week the amount needed had come in.

Barely able to contain their excitement, Benson and two of his elders called on the landowner on Friday afternoon and presented him with the money to buy the land.

"How did you get so much money in such a short time?" he asked, astounded.

"I told you that God would provide," Benson replied, "and our people believe God. They have given and pledged to purchase this land from you, because God wants a church to be built there. He will bless the people so they can pay their pledges and we can repay our loans."

The man drew up the legal documents with the help of lawyer K.S. Inneh and transferred the property to the little prayer group from Forestry Road. But they were soon to learn that this was only the beginning in their walk of faith.

A few days later the landlord who owned the storefront building they were renting notified Benson that they must move out in one month. And their final month's rent would be increased from twelve to twenty dollars. The young pastor knew they had only one way to go.

"God has helped us to raise money to buy land," he reminded the people. "Now we will continue to raise money every week to start our own building on that land."

Benson went to the fifty-by-one-hundred-foot plot of land and marked off an area forty by eighty feet for the foundation. Then he talked to a friendly contractor who agreed to begin work on the building.

The venture in faith seemed to be well under way when four of the five elders of the group called on Benson to protest the size of the building he had laid out. "Your eyes are too big," they said. "We feel the new church should seat about fifty people, and the building you have in mind will seat five hundred. We cannot have a hand in such a foolish project."

Benson listened to their argument, but he told the contractor to continue laying blocks for the foundation. One morning before going to his office, Benson arrived at the building site to find the contractor quite agitated. "Pastor Idahosa," he shouted over the noise of the cement mixer, "someone has removed some of the foundation blocks we laid yesterday! One of my workers says an elder of your church did it."

Benson walked over to inspect the damage, his indignation rising as he went. "Whoever removed these blocks will see this building erected, but will not worship here," he said prophetically. With that, he instructed the contractor to replace the blocks and continue work on the building as planned, then went on to his job at the shoe company.

The following Sunday Benson announced to the

congregation how some of the elders had removed some of the foundation blocks because they thought the building was too large. "I protest the action of these men," he declared. "On Tuesday I must go on a trip to Lagos for a meeting at the University of Lagos. I am appointing Elder Ogolo to be in charge of the church in my absence, but I expect work on the building to continue."

The special meetings in Lagos, about two hundred miles away, were planned to last through the next Sunday, but at three o'clock in the morning on that Sunday, Benson was suddenly awakened. *"There is a problem at home; you must go back immediately,"* the Lord told him.

There was no mistaking the message. Benson got up, dressed hurriedly, and hired a taxi to drive him back to Benin City. About eight o'clock the same morning he walked into the house to find Margaret sitting at the kitchen table weeping.

"What happened—why are you here?" she asked, startled. "I didn't expect you home until Monday."

Benson sat down beside her and took her hand in his. "The Lord told me to come home because there is a problem. What is it?"

"There was a meeting held yesterday," she replied, dropping her head and beginning to weep again. "You have been replaced as pastor of the church. The elders have elected Elder Ogolo."

"If the Lord wants to raise this man up, He will see that Elder Ogolo remains," Benson said, giving Margaret a handkerchief to wipe her tears. "But if it is not the Lord's doing, I will take my position. I am not fighting to be pastor, because I am still doing my job at Bata Shoe Company. Come, wash your face and let's go to church."

Benson fired up the motorcycle as Margaret took a seat on the rear fender, and they headed for Forestry Road. When they arrived at the storefront church about nine o'clock, the main service had not yet begun, but the new pastor had already taken his place behind the pulpit.

"Have you read today's newspaper?" the man asked as Benson approached the platform with his Bible under his arm. At this point only a few worshipers had gathered in the building.

"No, I haven't," Benson answered.

"You should read page five," Elder Ogolo continued. "There is the story that I have been ordained as the new pastor."

"I am grateful," Benson said, crossing his arms across his chest. "What do you want me to do?"

"Well . . . just take your seat in the congregation as an ordinary member of the congregation," Elder Ogolo answered, nervously wiping the perspiration from his face.

Benson gazed intently at the man for a few moments, then without another word turned and sat beside Margaret near the front.

Elder Ogolo began conducting the service, leading the songs and calling on another of the elders to lead in prayer. After the prayer, and before Elder Ogolo had time to resume his position behind the pulpit, Benson quickly walked up on the makeshift platform. "I am preaching to you today from John 3:16," he announced to the people, "—a sermon on the love of God."

The worshipers were surprised to see Benson come to the pulpit, because they thought he was still in Lagos. However, most of them did not yet know a new pastor had been elected. Elder Ogolo had planned to break the news in the service that morning.

Benson began his sermon, with his rival sitting behind him, hissing and pushing, trying to make him sit down. As he continued preaching about God's love, the people began to weep. The young preacher concluded by saying, "I'm not going to fight. If what God wanted to use me for is finished here, I cannot contest it. But people, I want you to know that when I went to Lagos I was still your pastor, and before I came home a new man had been appointed. I am no more your pastor after today."

When he started to walk off the platform the people all stood up and several of them called out, "You are our leader—you are our pastor. That man is not," pointing to Elder Ogolo.

"We will leave the matter in God's hands, and see what happens," Benson said.

He and Margaret returned home, and on Monday morning he went to his office in town as he usually did. But as the week progressed it seemed apparent that God was indeed directing the affairs of the little church on Forestry Road. On Tuesday, the son of the man who chaired the meeting in which Benson had been removed as pastor died of malaria. On Wednesday, the elder who had removed the foundation stones from the building site lost his daughter because of illness. On Thursday, the third protesting elder was taken to the hospital with tuberculosis. And on Friday, Elder Ogolo, the newly ordained pastor, was rushed to a hospital with a heart attack, then taken to Calabar for treatment. Within days the four troublemakers were removed. Benson resumed the pastoral duties of the little church.

The following week he conducted funerals for the two children who had died. He went to the hospital to pray for the elder with tuberculosis, but the man later died from the disease. After a time Elder Ogolo recovered, but he moved away from Benin City and got a job as a bricklayer.

Benson's position as pastor and leader was unquestionably vindicated. Yet his problems were far from over. There remained the responsibility of raising the necessary funds for moving ahead with the building project. It was a big undertaking for a small independent congregation with no financial backing. But Benson sensed in his spirit that he was moving in the right direction, and that somehow God would make a way.

Benson in one of his many crusades, which he conducts throughout Africa. He has ministered to crowds of more than 150,000.

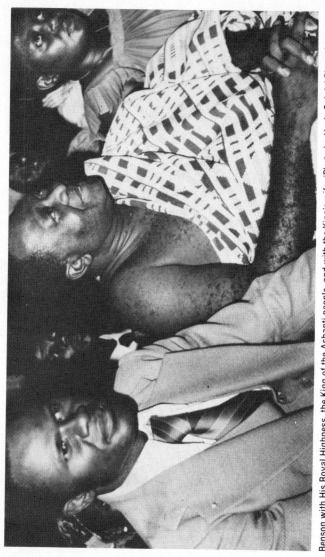

Benson with His Royal Highness, the King of the Ashanti people, and with the King's wife. (Photo by Uncle Gabriel Photo Agency.)

Benson when he was a manager for Bata Shoe Company. (Photo by S.O. Alonge, Ideal Photos Studio.)

Gordon and Freda Lindsay with their young protégé at the Christian Center in Dallas, Texas.

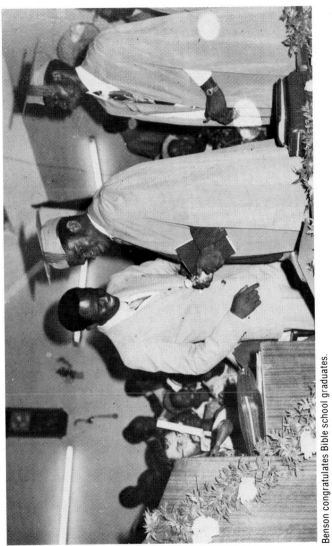
Benson congratulates Bible school graduates.

The young preacher begins his ministry.

Benson in his first suit (borrowed from Mr. Edward Ero), preparing to begin his preaching crusades. (Photo by Oxford Photos.)

Benson and Margaret on their wedding day.

The Rev. and Mrs. Benson A. Idahosa in Sweden during 1978.

Benson in his early days of ministry. (Photo by Oxford Photos.)

Benson with the Rev. S.G. Elton, in front of a part of the Miracle Centre complex. (Photo by Uncle Gabriel Photo Agency.)

Jim Bakker (second from left), host of "PTL Club," prays with Benson and Margaret during a recent broadcast.

Laying the foundation for the television studio. (Photo by Uncle Gabriel Colour Lab.)

Jim Bakker visits Benson in Nigeria.

The main church and headquarters of Miracle Centre. The sanctuary seats 4,000. (Photo by Uncle Gabriel Photo Agency.)

Inside Miracle Centre. "Redeemed Voices," the television choir, is in the foreground.

Parking space is at a premium at Miracle Centre. (Photo by Uncle Gabriel Photo Agency.)

Mrs. Gordon Lindsay visits Miracle Centre at time of dedication. (Photo by Uncle Gabriel Photo Agency.)

Benson gives a progress report to Governor Alli and his guests. (Photo by Uncle Gabriel Photo Agency.)

The Bible school dormitories, the office building, and the apartment house for missionaries.

# Opposition From the Enemy

Work on the building continued, and Benson kept a prodigious schedule as his responsibilities increased. He attended the early morning prayer meeting, then reported for work at the shoe company, taking breaks twice during the day to ride his motorcycle to the building site to be sure the work was running smoothly.

After leaving the office he went to the storefront building for a six o'clock, evening Bible class, then called on friends and relatives to tell them about the work. In ten weeks he had raised $7,500 and the building was almost finished. Some men donated labor, others gave concrete blocks and building supplies, and the carpenters agreed to do the roofing on credit.

The owner of the storefront building had extended his rental agreement one more month, but now the group was forced to vacate. The new Iyaro church still had no finished plaster, no roof, no seats and no windows, but the pastor and newly appointed elders declared the church to be open and began a revival meeting. The short dirt street leading from the main road had been without a name until the new church went up. Now it was officially named Church Street. And within the next few weeks Benson's vision of a crowd of people trooping from this street to the main road was a reality.

Early one evening when Benson was at the church in a small room alone, studying his Bible in preparation for the service, two men came to call on him. Benson had never seen them before. They introduced themselves; Benson greeted them and they sat down. They related several problems that were troubling them, and said they wanted special prayer.

"I'll be glad to pray with you," Benson said, "but first I need to talk with you about a few things." He sensed in his spirit that the men were not earnest seekers, but imposters sent to the church on an evil mission.

The young pastor began preaching the gospel to them, emphasizing the power of God against the occult and against evil. He gave examples from Scripture of Pharaoh, Nebuchadnezzar, and others who tried through the occult to put a curse upon God's people, and the consequences they suffered for it. "The same power of God is alive today to save those who call upon Him for salvation, but it is a serious thing to reject God's message and to oppose His servants."

He showed them in Scripture (Acts 13:4-12) the incident when the Apostle Paul went to preach to the proconsul of Paphos, and was opposed by Elymas the magician. "Paul discerned the man's evil intent, and put a temporary curse of blindness upon him," Benson said. "You see, the man of God had more power than the magician."

At these words, the eyes of one of the men bulged out in fear. "Let me tell you the truth," he said nervously, waving his hand to signal Benson to say no more. "We are not here for prayer. We are carrying charms with us, and we were sent here to tempt you to lay hands upon us, so that the curse on these charms would fall upon you and you would be paralyzed."

Then both men began crying out, "My body is burning—my body is burning! Deliver me!"

"Be burnt!" Benson commanded, and they cried out even more intensely. Then he laid hands on them and rebuked the power of the enemy, and the burning sensation stopped. In their state of fear, and at Benson's insistence, they confessed their sins and prayed a prayer of confession. At the pastor's urging, they stayed for the service that night, and he asked them to stand up and confess before the congregation. They went away from the church in quite a different state than they had expected, but Benson was never sure whether they made a total commitment to Jesus Christ, or whether they simply made a confession out of fear. Four days later one of the men died under mysterious circumstances; about three months later the other met a similar unexpected death.

The occult leader who had sent these men to put a curse of paralysis upon Benson came himself to the Iyaro church a short time after the first man's death. "I would like to find out what is the secret behind your life," the man said to Benson. "How is it you have such power?"

"It is the power of Jesus Christ," Benson explained. And he related some of the same examples from Scripture he had shared with his earlier visitors.

---

"I would like to have that kind of power," the man said.

Benson told him he could have it only if he committed himself totally to Jesus Christ and renounced his occult practices. The man was not willing to do this, but he was obviously impressed by reports he had heard of miraculous things happening in this place.

"Some of the other chiefs and I have had meetings to try to figure out what to do about you," he confided to the preacher. "We can't understand your power, or why none of our curses have been effective. We've tried everything to get rid of you, and nothing has worked."

"I've already told you the power comes from Jesus Christ," Benson said, pointing to the open pages of his Bible. "God's Word tells us that His power is stronger than any occult power—that is why your curses won't work."

The chief was so impressed with what he saw in Benson and at the Iyaro church that he hired twenty laborers and paid their salaries for one week to help complete the building. And he sent no more representatives to try to put a curse upon the pastor.

As the work at the Iyaro church continued to grow over the next few months, Benson realized the need for an advisor to whom he could go for spiritual counsel. When he started the small Bible study group on Forestry Road it had been under the guidance of the man through whose ministry he had been converted, Pastor Okpo. But Benson felt the work should remain independent, instead of becoming a part of a denomination. The exclusivism that seemed to go along with joining a denomination was not to his liking; yet he saw the value of having a spiritual overseer.

Alone in his bedroom one day he was praying about the problem when the Lord spoke to him very clearly: *"I have a servant in Ilesha named Elton whom you have never met. Go there and see him."* Benson even had a vision of what the man looked like; he was a white man with gray hair, about sixty years old.

Benson told one of his elders about the vision, and asked him to accompany him to Ilesha to find this man the Lord had told him to see. But before they got off on the trip, Benson saw a missionary he knew and mentioned that he was looking for a man named Elton, thinking the missionary might be able to give him directions.

"Oh, yes, I know him," the missionary said, "but you must not go to see him. He is a wicked man. Furthermore, he probably wouldn't let you into his compound, anyway."

"I must obey God," Benson responded. "I will find the man, and he will see me.

"I will talk to him and reconcile the two of you," Benson said confidently. And he went to the bus station to buy tickets.

The bus trip to Ilesha, one hundred and seventy-five miles northwest from Benin City, took about six hours over rough dirt roads. Upon arriving there, Benson began to inquire whether anyone knew a man named Elton. "I know a man who knows him," someone told him, and gave the two men an address. They hired a taxi and spent the last of their money to get to the man's house.

"Yes, I know Elton," the man told Benson. "Whatever you want to tell him, you can tell me and I will deliver the message."

"God didn't tell me to see you," Benson protested. "He told me to see Elton—He even showed me what he looks like."

"I'll make a phone call for you," the man agreed.

Benson and his church elder could overhear one end of the conversation: "Hello—Brother Elton?—I have a stubborn young man here from Benin City named Benson Idahosa. He wants to see you—says God told him to come up here and find you."

After a brief silence the man hung up, turned to Benson and said, "Well, he says for you to come and see him. But I am not sure that I should tell you how to find his place."

"I want you to lay hands on me and pray that God will show me the way," Benson said.

A bit bewildered, the man agreed, and Benson knelt in front of him. After the prayer Benson got up to leave, but suddenly turned to the man and said, "I have a feeling in my spirit that God wants you to drive me to Elton's place."

"I don't want to go," the man protested.

"You will go, sir," Benson replied. "You have prayed, and I believe you are a man of God."

The three of them got in the man's car and started out, but halfway to their destination the man rebelled completely. "I am not going any further," he declared, stopping the car.

"Okay, if you will not take us there, then give us the

---

money to continue by taxi," Benson asked.

The man gave them two shillings (about twenty-four cents) and dropped them at the side of the road. Benson hailed a taxi and they continued their journey. When the driver pulled up at the gate, a white man was standing there waiting for them. "You are the man from Benin City, aren't you?" he said.

"Yes, and you are Brother Elton," Benson replied, offering his hand. "You are the man God showed me. The Lord has called me to come see you and ask you to be my father to lead me in the ministry."

Elton shook his hand warmly. "Come inside," he invited. "We have many things to talk about."

When they were settled in the parlor of the mission house, Mrs. Elton served tea and biscuits to the guests from Benin City. "I have heard of you for months and have wanted to meet you," the older man said to Benson. "I am so glad the Lord has brought you here."

Benson smiled and put his teacup down on the table. "The devil put many obstacles in our path to keep us from finding you, but I know this is God's will," he said.

Elton listened as Benson and the elder described the work in Benin City and shared what God was doing in their midst. "We will be grateful for any advice, or for any kind of help," Benson said enthusiastically. "Our people and friends in the community have sacrificed to give to the building fund, but we will owe for the roof."

"One thing I can do is to help you get funds for the roofing costs," the older man volunteered. "A friend of mine in the States, Gordon Lindsay, has a missions organization which assists groups like yours."

At the end of their visit the men concluded that they should get together at least once a month so that Elton could give advice and direction to the ministry of the church. They would alternate meetings between Ilesha and Benin City.

Elton drove them into town to catch the bus back to Benin City, and gave Benson an offering of seven pounds (about sixteen dollars) when he said goodbye.

Bumping over the ruts and bumps on the road home, the young preacher rejoiced that God had helped him find the man in his vision. But he could not possibly know at this point that through Brother Elton another door was about to open.

## 11

# A New Beginning

For as long as he could remember, Benson had had a voracious appetite for learning. Since becoming a Christian his desire was to study and understand the Bible, but he had had no opportunity to enroll as a resident student in a mission Bible school. Somehow he obtained a copy of *Christ For The Nations* magazine published in Dallas, Texas, and read about a correspondence course called "The Life and Teachings of Christ." He wrote the editor, the Rev. Gordon Lindsay, and asked to be enrolled.

Several weeks later he was thrilled to receive a packet of books and study materials. The novice preacher plunged into the studies like a starving man who had just discovered an unlimited source of bread. He sent a letter of thanks to his benefactor. "Some day I hope to meet you in person," he wrote.

One day early in 1971 Benson received a letter from Brother Elton in Ilesha. "I am bringing Gordon Lindsay to visit you in Benin City," the message read. "He has come to Nigeria to visit some of the churches helped through Christ For The Nations. Since I obtained help from his organization for the new roof on your church, I want him to see the work there at Iyaro. We will arrive the afternoon of March 21."

Benson, exuberant over the news, called his elders together and told them of the letter. Despite having only two days' notice, the elders decided a special meeting should be called for the occasion. They quickly printed invitation cards and distributed them all over the Iyaro district.

On the appointed day, about 250 people gathered in the still-unfinished church and waited almost two hours for the visitors. When Brother Lindsay and Brother Elton finally arrived, they were greeted by applause and cheers from the crowd and a firm handshake and wide grin from the young pastor and his wife, Margaret. The brightly colored Nigerian dresses and headpieces, the smiling faces, the spirited singing and handclapping combined to present a panorama of color, rhythm and motion. As Benson led the people in praising the Lord, it seemed the new roof was almost lifted off the building.

The two visitors entered into the spirit of worship, thoroughly enjoying the experience. While the meeting was in progress, Brother Elton turned to Gordon Lindsay and said, "I believe this man is going to be a key man in the work of God in Nigeria—I think we ought to ordain him to the ministry."

"Yes, I agree," Brother Lindsay replied, nodding emphatically. "I think God has raised him up to do a mighty work in this country."

Stepping behind the pulpit, Brother Elton introduced his guest, Gordon Lindsay, and explained to the people that the two of them had agreed to ordain the pastor to the ministry. Benson knelt at the altar as the older men anointed him with oil and prayed a prayer of ordination. To the natural eye, the exercise may have seemed merely a ceremonial formality for the young preacher in the rather frayed and ill-fitting suit. But to the spiritual eye, here was a young prophet being clothed with the mantle of Elijah—a double portion of power for the ministry to which God had called him.

The next morning before departing, Gordon Lindsay said to Brother Elton, "I believe Benson ought to come to the United States to go to Bible school. If he will come to Dallas, I will give him a scholarship to the school we've just opened at Christ For The Nations."

It seemed like an impossible dream—the opportunity to go to Bible school in Dallas! What an invaluable addition to the study he had already done by correspondence. This was not Benson's first invitation to go abroad for training. Bata Shoe Company had tried for some time to send him to a college in Essex, England, for administrative training, but he had been unwilling to leave his post of ministry to further his business career. However, Bible training held an irresistible appeal. This offer Benson would accept.

The directors at Bata had already applied for his passport in the hope he would go to England. When he asked for leave from his job to go to the States, they readily agreed and even volunteered to complete all the paper work for him. Within a few months he had his passport, visa, airline ticket and confirmed reservations. His leave from work was with full pay, so he and Margaret would not have to depend solely upon her low teacher's salary.

In August, 1971, he charged the board of elders with the responsibility of looking after the church in his absence, and preached his farewell sermon. The most difficult part was leaving Margaret. She had matured in her Christian experience and had truly become a help-meet to him in the ministry. The increasing pressure from their families because of their childlessness had only served to draw them closer together.

"You're really the only friend I have," Margaret told him tearfully as she watched him snap shut his suitcases. "I know you must take this opportunity, but I hate to see you leave."

Benson held her close for several moments, then prayed with her. "The Lord will be with you every moment I am gone," he said tenderly, wiping away the tears that glistened on her cheeks. "He will strengthen and help both of us until we're together again. Remember, He has promised we will have children, and He will not fail us."

One of the elders took them by car to the airport, where friends and relatives were waiting to bid Benson farewell. Waving goodbye to the crowd lining the edge of the tarmac, Benson embarked on the journey that would irrevocably change the course of his ministry. He settled back for his first-ever flight and contemplated what lay ahead as the plane went soaring into the clouds. Little did he know that this was the first of literally hundreds of airline flights he would experience in the future as his ministry would take him to dozens of countries of the world. For the time being, a flight to the United States seemed a momentous undertaking.

The fourteen-hour journey from Benin City to Lagos to New York City to Dallas put him into a totally different world. Coming from a country where blacks were the majority and whites a small minority, he found the situation reversed in the United States. White faces seemed to surround the young Nigerian, as in colorful native dress he made his way through the bustling crowds at John F. Kennedy Airport in New York.

Arriving at Love Field in Dallas in the early evening, he was bewildered about what to do. No representative from CFNI was there to meet him because the exact time of his arrival was so uncertain.

"Could I drive you where you need to go?" a fellow passenger asked. "My car is here at the airport." The woman, a professor at a Dallas university, was returning with two of her colleagues from a New York convention. Benson gratefully accepted her offer and gave her the address of Christ For The Nations Institute.

As the car sped over the freeway, Benson was amazed at the size of the city surrounding him. They had been driving for more than twenty minutes, and still had not reached the CFNI campus nor the edge of the city! The metropolis stretched for miles in every direction, crisscrossed by freeways filled with speeding cars. They finally got off the freeway, turned down Conway Street, and stopped in front of a large yellow brick apartment complex. It seemed to be the only building on the block showing any signs of life.

"Let me ask someone where I am to go," Benson said, getting out of the car. Just then a young woman came out of the entrance of the building.

———

"Are you the new student from Nigeria?" she asked, noticing his brightly colored embroidered shirt and trousers.

"Yes," Benson answered. "This is Christ For The Nations, isn't it?"

"Welcome! We've been expecting you—Brother Lindsay told us you were coming. Come, meet the apartment manager. . . ."

Within minutes Benson was climbing the stairs to the quarters that would be his home for the coming months. "Your roommate has already arrived," the manager explained, knocking on a door at the top of the stairs.

A tall, blond young man opened the door. "You must be Benson!" he said warmly, extending his hand. "Please come in—I've been looking forward to meeting you. I'm Wayne Blikstad." Suddenly students were coming from every direction to greet the new arrival from Nigeria. Benson strained to understand what they were saying to him. They all spoke English, but it sounded so different from what he was accustomed to hearing back home—the considerable contrast between a British accent and a stateside midwestern accent!

When the excitement subsided, the two roommates settled down to get acquainted. Though coming from diverse backgrounds—one a black man from Nigeria, the other a white American from a middle-class family in Minnesota—they had the same goal: to study the Bible and seek God's guidance for their lives. Their common goal and common faith instantly made them brothers.

"Father," Benson prayed before dropping off to sleep

that night, "help me to learn from this experience in Dallas all that you have in store for me. . . ." At the time he had no idea of the things that would be involved in the answer to that prayer.

Benson spent the first few days adjusting to the time change and becoming familiar with his new surroundings. At first he went out for most of his meals, but then discovered he could buy chicken, rice and eggs and other staples cheaper than they were in Nigeria, and he began preparing his own food. He often invited other students to share the meals he fixed, which they loved to do.

One difficulty he had was in comprehending the size and scope of his host country. He had never been beyond the south central region of Nigeria, so he barely had a grasp of the size of his own nation. Now he was in a country ten times the size of Nigeria.

He had brought with him several letters to deliver for friends who had relatives living in the United States. With the help of another student, he phoned a fellow Nigerian living in Los Angeles and told him he had a letter for the man from his father. "Can you come pick up the letter this evening?" Benson asked.

"Where are you staying?" the man inquired, not realizing it was a long-distance call.

"I'm at Christ For The Nations in Dallas, Texas," Benson answered. "I'm staying in one of the dormitories here."

"Dallas!" the man exclaimed. "But that's a long way from here!"

"Well, can you take a taxi?" Benson asked.

"No, no—you don't understand. Dallas is fifteen hundred miles from Los Angeles," the friend explained. "You must mail the letter to me."

Benson quickly learned that all the letters he had hoped to deliver by hand were to cities a great distance from Dallas, so he was forced to mail every one. He had no idea at the time that one day in the future his ministry would take him to forty of the fifty states, and only then would he grasp the size of this huge country.

The scorching heat and high humidity of August in Texas was reminiscent of the hot weather in Nigeria. But except for the climate, there were few similarities. The most shocking reality was adjusting to the discovery that he was the only black person in the group of more than a hundred students. It was his first experience living with white people.

However, adjusting to the spiritual climate of CFNI was no problem! On Sunday afternoon Benson and Wayne walked the short distance to the building called Christian Center for the opening rally of the new school year—only the second year of the school's operation. They arrived early and went into the prayer room where other students had already gathered. The sound of united prayer was like music to his ears, and Benson heartily joined in.

Then the two roommates found seats in the auditorium as the meeting began with music and worship. Including the students and outside visitors, about three hundred people were in the room, but judging from the sound of their exuberant worship, it could have been a thousand. Benson did not know most of the songs, but he took part in the handclapping and praising, and tried to learn some of the choruses.

Gordon Lindsay was conductng the meeting. "Benson Idahosa has just arrived from Nigeria," he announced, "and is the first foreign student to come to Christ For The Nations Institute." He motioned for Benson to come to the platform. "I believe God's hand is upon this young man to reach his nation for Christ. We are pleased to have him with us as a student."

Benson was overwhelmed with gratitude as he shared with the people how Gordon Lindsay had ordained him to the ministry and invited him to attend Bible school in Dallas. "I thank God for Dad Lindsay and his vision for the world," he said with his inimitable Nigerian accent. "I am here to learn everything I can about how to minister in the power of the Holy Spirit. So many people in my country are held in the bondage of darkness; only the power of the Holy Spirit can set them free. I want God to use me to help them find that freedom."

From the first day of classes, it was evident the young man from Africa was no ordinary student. He took copious notes during the lectures, and seemed to absorb and assimilate the truth from every lesson. But his most striking quality was the urgency and power with which he prayed. During the early morning hours, his roommate and nearby neighbors could hear Benson interceding for his country and his people. The need for reaching them with the gospel of Jesus Christ seemed to weigh continually upon him.

Another thing his fellow students noticed was that

he wrote scores of letters; he sensed it was extremely important to maintain close contact with Margaret and with the elders of the church. He especially felt the need to encourage his wife. "Don't be discouraged," he wrote her. "Since arriving in Dallas God has assured me that whatever He has promised, He will do—if our faith does not fail. Not only will we have a child, but God has given me a name for him: 'Emmanuel.' And God will fulfill His promise."

Benson soon learned that yet another aspect of his training was to take place outside the classroom. As a foreign student on scholarship, he was required to work each afternoon to fulfill the work assignment given him. The office manager of Christ For The Nations explained that it was his duty to look after the grounds and parking area around the office building and Christian Center.

Each weekday afternoon the young African worked outdoors watering the shrubs, picking up litter, and trying to keep the grounds in good order. But he noticed that other students who worked in the afternoons had jobs inside in the air-conditioned office. "I suppose they gave me this job working outdoors just because I'm black," he figured, as a cloud of inferiority began settling over him. The weather became colder, the gusts of wind stronger, and Benson grew increasingly to suspect that being black meant serving in the lowliest of positions. And he chafed under it.

One day, just as he had swept up a pile of litter and was about to put it in the trash bin, a gust of wind blew it all over the parking lot. "Lord!" Benson exclaimed, leaning on the broom handle and looking up into the Texas sky. "Is this why you brought me to this place—to sweep the grounds? How can this help me in the ministry?"

In that quiet moment of desperation he seemed to hear a voice say, *"Sweep it up again."* And he did.

A few days later Benson was sitting in class listening to Chuck Flynn, a guest lecturer visiting the school. At the close of the lesson while the students were waiting quietly in prayer, the speaker began to prophesy:

A servant of the Lord is here who is feeling forgotten and neglected; the enemy is assailing you. But do not be discouraged nor feel abandoned. God has brought you here to equip you and use you for His glory. And you will go back to your country with a flame of fire in your soul.

Since Benson was the only foreign student enrolled at that time, there was little doubt the prophecy was directed to him. He jumped to his feet and cried out. Brother Flynn called him forward for prayer, and a group of students gathered with him at the front. As they wept and prayed together, Benson knew he was set free from the enemy's influence. Never again would he feel subservient because of the color of his skin. At last he realized that God is gloriously colorblind!

From that time he became more active in praying for students and ministering to people who came to the public meetings at Christ For The Nations. The students were drawn to him, and often sought him out for counsel. And an interesting phenomenon began to accompany his ministry. Very often when he prayed for an individual, he or she would fall to the floor, "slain in the Spirit." Benson had seen this happen when others were ministering. Though he did not fully understand it, he noticed it almost always happened when he felt a strong anointing during ministry. He knew it was truly the work of the Holy Spirit.

# 12

# Returning With a Vision

On his last visit with brother Elton before leaving Nigeria, Benson had gotten the names of pastors and churches in the midwestern United States whom the older man felt he should contact while in Dallas. Benson had written to them, and some wrote back inviting him to their churches for weekend ministry. In addition, other students who were involved in weekend ministry often asked him to go along, so he stayed busy traveling to areas around Dallas.

One weekend in Ada, Oklahoma, someone gave him a book about world evangelism written by T.L. Osborn. Benson was quite familiar with this man's writings; for several years he had been ordering tracts from T.L. Osborn and distributing them on his preaching trips to the villages around Benin City. But as he began reading this book on his way back to Dallas that weekend in late November, it disturbed him profoundly.

The book cited the rate at which the world's population is growing, and noted that the rate at which souls were being won to Christ was far below the population growth rate. The statistics were astonishing. Benson read:

---

Right now it is a fair estimate that there are *one and a half billion souls* who have never once heard the gospel. This represents over half of the world's population, and includes tribespeople who speak some 2,000 different languages! The world is hurtling to a lost eternity at a frightening rate.

. . . Population increases by over 150,000 daily or nearly *60 million* annually, with only about two million of this increase reached in any degree with the gospel. Thirty times more souls are born than converts made. A quarter of all nations, a third of the earth's surface and half of the world's population is under communist influence.

. . . The time has come for Christians to enter this vast human harvest field with renewed vigor and dedication. If more laborers do not volunteer for greater soulwinning, we shall lose the world—and our liberty to evangelize.[1]

For two or three days after returning to classes at Christ For The Nations Institute, Benson wept and prayed and fasted over the message of that book. In his mind's eye he could see millions of his own countrymen in Nigeria who were enslaved by heathenism and juju worship, dying without salvation through Christ. And so few, comparatively speaking, were attempting to reach them with the gospel. His soul was burning with the challenge to take the message of life to his own people. How could he possibly remain in school while Nigerians perished? He felt like the prophet of old who

---

[1]T.L. Osborn, *Soulwinning: Out Where the Sinners Are* (1966), pp. 67-69.

---

wrote, "There is in my heart as it were a burning fire shut up in my bones, and I am weary with holding it in, and I cannot" (Jer. 20:9 RSV).

Finally he sought out Gordon Lindsay to share with him the burden he felt, and to tell him about the book he had read. He also shared the vision God had shown him three years earlier of the dead tree that came to life. "I must return to Nigeria right away," Benson told his teacher. "The need for evangelism is so urgent; yet I'm getting reports that attendance at the church in Benin City is dropping. I cannot stay away any longer."

To his great relief, "Dad" Lindsay understood perfectly. "We'll give you the books for the courses planned for the rest of the school year," Brother Lindsay told him. "You can complete the studies on your own."

"I've already read most of the books for this semester," Benson said, "but I want to continue my studies when I return to Nigeria."

"The most valuable lessons you've learned here have not been out of the textbooks," Brother Lindsay said, smiling and patting his student on the shoulder. "You've learned the importance and power of prayer, and I believe your ministry—which was already anointed—has been lifted to a new level of faith. When you return to Nigeria, you will find that these lessons are truly the most valuable of all."

Word that Benson was leaving school before the Christmas break spread quickly across the campus. He had won the hearts of both students and staff members, and they were surprised and sad to hear the news. A few tried to dissuade him, but quickly saw he was firm in his conviction that he must return to his country.

Students and other friends began giving him gifts of every description to take with him back to Nigeria. By the time the day of his departure dawned, he had what looked like a mountain of luggage to take home with him. Before going to chapel on that final morning, Benson's roommate gave him a beautiful leatherbound Bible with his name stamped in gold on the front cover.

Benson fingered the smooth, supple leather and riffled through the pages, suddenly remembering those days years ago on Uncle Joseph's farm when he had struggled so hard to learn how to read. "Thank you, Wayne," he said, hugging the white man with whom he had lived. "I pray God will enable me to use this Bible to preach to my people with a greater anointing then ever before."

"He will, Benson—He will," Wayne replied, his voice husky with emotion as he hugged the tall African.

The chapel service that morning was a commissioning service for the first foreign student to be sent back to his home country from Christ For The Nations Institute. Gordon Lindsay laid hands on Benson and prayed that a double portion of the power of the Holy Spirit would rest upon his ministry. "We expect to hear a good report when you get back to Nigeria," Brother Lindsay said as he shook hands and told his student goodbye. Benson had no way of knowing that was the last time he was to see his teacher alive, but he would be forever grateful to "Dad" Lindsay for his expression of confidence.

While riding to the airport in the school van, Benson looked out the back window and saw that several carloads of students had cut classes to follow him to the airport for a final send-off. He created quite a scene at the check-in counter in his brightly colored Nigerian regalia and hat, surrounded by enthusiastic students helping to carry what looked to be enough baggage for five or six people.

When he checked in for the flight Benson was shocked to learn that the airline intended to charge him several hundred dollars for overweight baggage. This was a detail of international travel he had not experienced before. "May I talk to the manager, please?" He asked the clerk. Immediately the students who were there to see him off began to pray.

When the manager arrived on the scene, Benson explained that he was a Bible school student returning to his home country of Nigeria. "These extra bags contain books and gifts my friends have given to be taken back to my people," he explained. "I cannot afford to pay these extra charges; is there anything you can do to help me?"

The manager looked at Benson's ticket and at the bags piled on the scale, thought it over for a few moments, then said to the clerk, "Okay, waive the extra charges." So the preacher's return trip started with the miracle of checking excess baggage free of charge, and ended in Nigeria when he went through customs without paying any duty on the goods.

During the trip home Benson pondered over the situation that awaited him in Benin City. The church attendance had dropped, despite the elder's very best efforts. He knew that what was needed to build the work up again was strong, anointed leadership. But he remembered the crisis of leadership the church had suffered at the beginning of the building program. Would such a thing happen again? Would the people regard him as a "foreigner" after his absence? What was their response likely to be?

During the entire trip Benson asked God to give him wisdom to cope with whatever situation awaited him. "Lord, you promised to send me back to my country with a flame of fire in my soul," he prayed. "Help my people to recognize it, and to be willing to follow in the direction you lead me."

After arriving in Lagos and clearing customs, he phoned Margaret in Benin City and told her when he would arrive there. She notified the church elders, who would in turn inform the congregation.

The one-hour flight from Lagos to Benin city seemed to take forever, but at last the plane landed and taxied to a stop on the tarmac. Benson looked out the window to see many relatives and scores of people from the Iyaro church waiting at the bottom of the steps to greet him. At the head of the crowd were the church elders and Margaret, smiling and waving and looking even more beautiful than he remembered her.

He waited impatiently for the door to open, then bounded down the steps to greet his people. But an astonishing thing happened. One by one, as various ones came to shake their pastor's hand, they were slain in the Spirit right on the tarmac. A number of people were filled with the Holy Spirit and began speaking in tongues. Benson would turn to grasp another hand being extended, and another church member would fall down—until about twenty people had "gone down under the power." No one understood exactly what was happening, but there was no question but that their pastor had arrived home with a powerful anointing of the Holy Spirit upon him. And from that first day back on Nigerian soil, the fire in his soul burned brighter and with greater intensity than it ever had before.

# 13

# What Price Unity?

Once the excitement of returning home had subsided, Benson turned his attention to the desire that had compelled him to leave school early—evangelizing his own people. He began by scheduling a service every night in the Iyaro church and urging the Christians to invite their families and friends. The people responded eagerly; they were delighted to have their pastor back. During his absence the attendance had dropped to less than two hundred, but it began to increase. The electric, dynamic presence of the Holy Spirit was evident every time Benson stepped behind the pulpit.

He reported to his superiors at Bata Shoe Company to explain why he was back sooner than expected. He learned that during his absence the company had given him two promotions and a salary increase. As a regular policy they allowed an employee two weeks of leave when he returned from an overseas assignment, with the possibility of another two-week extension. They agreed to give him a full four weeks of leave, which meant he could devote his full attention to the church.

"Surely the other pastors in Benin City must feel the same burden to reach the lost that I feel," he reasoned. "I'll talk to some of them and enlist their help." He talked to the pastor of one of the larger denominational churches in town, who agreed to call a meeting at his church of all the pastors in the city. When the men were assembled, Benson stood up and appealed to them to cooperate in a joint evangelistic effort to reach Benin City for Christ. And he suggested they form a fellowship of evangelists to reach all of Nigeria. The pastors did not actually oppose his ideas, but neither did they express any enthusiasm for them. In principle the men felt they should have unity among themselves, but settling on a unified course of action proved to be more difficult than Benson had anticipated. It seemed every suggestion he made bounced back in his face, and instead of encouraging his enthusiasm, the men were suspicious of it. It was Benson's first experience at trying to do the Lord's work by means of a committee. The meeting finally ended without any conclusive action being agreed upon.

Bitterly disappointed, Benson returned home to ponder his next move. The vision he had seen four years earlier burned in his memory. He knew without question that God had called him to evangelism, but he could not understand why most other pastors did not share his zeal. He really felt a unified effort would be most effective; but if no one cooperated, should he do it alone? Picking up the book on soulwinning, he leafed through its pages and read:

. . . The man who succeeds learns to live with criticism. He must adopt the right philosophy about criticism. . . . People usually only criticize the man out front. The failing man, the non-successful man, the orthodox run-of-the-mill commands no attention. He is ordinary. He's going no place. He doesn't force men to think new.

. . . There are two classes of people: those with problems and those with solutions. The man with solutions is the man in demand. Anybody can create problems, discuss them, analyze them, categorize them. Only the thinker—the creator— the man of action has the solutions.

. . . *Don't fight the problem; get on with the solution.*[1]

He knew evangelism was the solution. The fire still burned in his own soul, and he resolved not to allow the pastors' indifference to extinguish it. He called his elders and Brother Elton together to discuss a plan for evangelism. Using a map of Nigeria, they divided the country into four sections and decided to schedule an evangelistic crusade in each section, beginning with Benin City in what was then called the Midwestern Region. They booked Ogbe Stadium for five days, February 25-29, 1972.

Such a thing had never been done in Benin City. The soccer stadium seated sixty thousand people at that time, and there had never been a truly large Christian gathering of any kind. But Benson and his people took a giant step of faith, and began publicizing the crusade and inviting people to come. They ran ads on the radio,

---

[1]T.L. Osborn, *Soulwinning: Out Where the Sinners Are* (1966), pp. 106-7.

---

drove a sound truck through the city announcing the crusade, and distributed posters and handbills under the name of "Christ For The Nations Evangelistic Association, Nigeria." An air of expectancy began to build as opening night approached.

No one knew what the response of the community would be, but Benson was confident he was moving in God's will. On the appointed Friday night he was thrilled to see about five thousand people gathered in the stadium. Granted, they filled only a fraction of the seats available, but it was a significant beginning.

The young pastor preached a strong salvation message, then appealed to his listeners to accept Jesus Christ as Savior and Lord of their lives. Scores of people began to respond, streaming to the front of the platform for prayer. Workers from the Iyaro church prayed and counseled with the new converts, and recorded names and addresses for follow-up. Then Benson announced he would pray for the sick, and another group of people went forward. Many miracles of healing took place in response to the prayer of faith, as the religious community looked on with a somewhat jaundiced eye.

Word spread throughout the city that something was happening at Ogbe Stadium. The next night even more people came to the meeting, and the crowds grew nightly to about ten thousand people for the final service. By the time the crusade was over several hundred had been born again, and many had been healed of various maladies and diseases. Attendance at the Iyaro church increased until the building was filled to capacity every Sunday, with people standing outside looking through the doors and windows.

Benson smiled ruefully when he remembered the accusation that his vision was "too big" when the Iyaro church was built to accommodate five hundred people. Now the Sunday attendance was more than seven hundred, and they couldn't crowd into the building. He checked around the community and got permission from the government to use the tennis courts at nearby Edo College. So the Sunday service—from nine in the morning to two o'clock in the afternoon—was held on the tennis courts, and the week-night Bible studies continued at the Iyaro church.

Many of the men and women who had accepted Christ during the crusade were coming regularly to the Bible study sessions, and were making rapid spiritual progress. Many of them were educated, professional people who now, since their lives had been transformed, wanted to learn all they could from the Word of God. Benson could see that his vision was beginning to be fulfilled. Those who had been set free from their heavy loads were being strengthened, and were now able to help others who needed deliverance. Some of the crusade converts were already becoming leaders in the work.

One was a man in the Nigerian army who had also been a member of a secret cult. After his conversion he formed a gospel team made up of military men called "Soldiers of Christ." They went all over Nigeria preaching the gospel and winning hundreds of converts among other soldiers. These men had opportunities to witness wherever their military assignments took them—

often to remote areas where no preacher had been.

Up to this time the Iyaro church had operated as an independent group with Benson as pastor, Brother Elton as his advisor, and a board of elders chosen from the congregation. What had begun as a small Bible study group had grown to a large congregation. The body was planning to sponsor six crusades a year in various parts of the country and to establish branch churches, and the Bible study program was expanding to a one-year Bible college with a British missionary appointed as principal. It seemed wise that they should register with the government, so in 1974 the leaders incorporated under the name Church of God Mission, International. At the time Benson and his co-workers were planning a few crusades in other nearby African countries, but no one dreamed that within a few short years Benson's ministry would reach out to over sixty-six nations of the world. The decision to include the word *international* proved to be truly providential.

The work of evangelism and overseeing the work of the church and Bible school by this time had become an all-consuming task for Benson. Although he had assistance from missionaries and staff members who helped carry the load, he was unquestionably captain of the team. He knew he could never return to a secular job. One day he called on his superiors at Bata Shoe Company and told them he could not come back to work. They refused his resignation and continued paying his salary, hoping desperately he would someday agree to return. But they simply did not understand the young preacher's motivation. Finally, he made a trip to

Lagos to the head office of the company and asked them to please stop sending his salary checks, and they agreed.

In the months following, Benson conducted crusades in the other three sections of Nigeria—the Eastern Region, Western Region, and Northern Region—with results similar to those of the Benin City Crusade. Local pastors did the follow-up work on new converts, and several new congregations were established.

Benson knew beyond doubt that the enemy's stronghold was being damaged when the occult community began to oppose his crusade efforts. One day while the crusade in the Eastern Region was in progress, a knock came at the door of the hotel room where he was staying. He opened the door to find two strange men standing there, almost cowering in fear.

"Reverend Idahosa, may we have a word with you please?" they asked.

"Yes, come in," Benson answered. "What brings you here?"

Hesitantly at first, they began to tell him that they had been hired by occult leaders in Benin City to follow him to this crusade, and to assassinate him when he stood before the crowd to preach.

"We were at the meeting last night with a gun," one man said, "and we intended to carry out our assignment. But we began listening to your message, and when you invited people to accept Christ, we went forward and prayed the sinner's prayer."

Both men were now extremely agitated. "We are afraid to go back to Benin City," the second one said.

"When the man who hired us finds out about this, he will have us killed. What shall we do?"

"First, you must recognize that the power of Christ is stronger than the power of the devil," Benson explained. "If Christ lives within you, they cannot touch you. That is why you were not able to kill me—the Bible says, '. . . greater is he that is in you, than he that is in the world' (1 John 4:4). I will pray for you that the Lord will give you boldness to witness to those men when you go back and report what has happened."

They knelt as Benson laid hands on them and prayed, then the two returned to Benin City. As expected, their employer was angry when he heard the unexpected news. But when the men witnessed to him and told him of the miracles they saw happen under this preacher's ministry, he was too fearful to lay a hand on them.

As the crusades progressed, and Benson and Margaret saw literally hundreds of people coming into the Kingdom, they rejoiced and praised God. But their joy was truly complete when they learned that at last Margaret was expecting a child. Although a gynecologist had told her that she had a chronic disorder that would prevent her from ever having a baby, his diagnosis was proven wrong. Margaret was ecstatic when they knew she was indeed pregnant. "I knew God would not fail us," Benson said with a broad smile. "We shall have a son, and his name will be Faith Emmanuel Benson."

And he was right. On December 22, 1972, their son was born, just slightly more than a year from the time the Lord had reaffirmed His promise to Benson while he was a student at Christ For The Nations Institute. They named the baby according to plan—Faith Emmanuel Benson—and decided to call him "Feb" for short, using the first letter of each of his three names. At last, both families were pleased. A son had been born. God had answered the prayer of faith.

But the pastors in town were not pleased. While the Iyaro congregation had been growing at a phenomenal rate, many of the other churches in town had seen a noticeable drop in attendance. Benson was beginning to get complaints. It was now early in 1973, about a year since the Benin City crusade, and the pastors called another meeting to discuss unity. Benson went at their invitation, not really knowing what to expect. A spokesman stood up in the meeting and said the pastors in the city wanted to unite and work together. The men around him were all nodding their heads in agreement as the man spoke.

"Why are they suddenly so agreeable?" Benson wondered. "When I spoke to them about unity last year all they could do was tell me why my ideas wouldn't work. . . ."

Just then the speaker riveted his gaze upon Benson, and the young pastor realized everyone in the room was looking directly at him. "Pastor Idahosa, we all know that many of our church members have been attending your church. Now, if we are going to have unity, you must return all those members to their original churches. You've been stealing our sheep."

Benson was nonplussed. They were obviously waiting for him to say something, and he well knew what they wanted to hear. "Lord, help me!" he prayed silently. "I need your wisdom for this situation."

The tall preacher rose to his full height, squared his shoulders, and looked around the room. He was a commanding figure in his dark suit, crisp white shirt, and dark tie; he was in no hurry to respond. At that moment, he sensed that the Holy Spirit had put in his mind exactly what he was to say.

"Gentlemen," he said slowly and deliberately, "we do not steal sheep at the Church of God Mission. But we do grow grass—and we won't deny any hungry sheep who wants to graze." Then he sat down and awaited their response.

The room was silent for a moment, then an angry pastor stood up. "What do you mean by 'growing grass'?" he asked.

"The grass is the Word of God," Benson replied calmly.

"Are you saying we don't preach the Word of God in our churches?" another man demanded.

"No, I didn't say that. But we do preach the full gospel at our church," Benson responded. "Jesus said, '. . . him that cometh to me I will in no wise cast out.'[2] Jesus never turned anyone away, and we won't turn any sheep away, either. We're only trying to reach the lost through the ministry of the Word, and through evangelistic crusades."

"We're not trying to stop your crusades," one pastor said, "We just want you to return our church members.

---

[2] John 6:37

If you are really interested in unity—as you said last year you were—you will cooperate with us as a witness to the entire community."

"I'm not going to tell the sheep where they should graze," Benson said firmly. "Whoever God is with will keep the sheep." As far as he was concerned, the subject was closed. But the pastors had planned their strategy carefully. About that time a man who had been sitting at the back of the room confronted Benson and told him he was a journalist with one of the local newspapers.

"If you don't cooperate, I'll put this story on the front page and ruin you," he threatened. "I've ruined other prominent men in this country, and I can do it to you, too. In three months your church will be forgotten by everyone."

"You can write anything you like," Benson said, quite unperturbed. "I've only done what God called me to do, and I make no apology for it. As I said, wherever the power of God is, the sheep will stay there." With that, he walked out of the meeting.

He arrived home to find Margaret sitting in the bedroom nursing their infant son. Tossing his coat on a chair and stretching across the bed to relax for a few minutes, he poured out the story of what had happened at the pastor's meeting. It was a comfort to speak his mind to Margaret and know she would listen and understand.

"Well, no one said it would be easy," she said quietly, holding Feb against her shoulder and patting him gently on the back. "But if God is with you, that's all that matters. You don't need the approval of men."

True to his word, the journalist began writing and publishing articles in the local newspaper in an attempt to discredit Benson's ministry. Though the articles never mentioned his name, it was clear that Benson was the target. The writer presented all the classical arguments against healing and miracles, saying those who believed in healing were not truly Christian, and that miracles and healings had taken place during the apostolic age only to prove that Christ had risen from the dead. "A true Christian knows that such things ended when the last apostle died," he wrote. Then he tried a smear campaign by accusing "this pastor" of being a subversive agent with the American CIA (Central Intelligence Agency) and receiving foreign aid under false pretenses.

Benson never answered the charges; he simply kept on doing what he had been doing. The primary effect the articles had was to make people curious enough to come out to the meetings to see for themselves what was happening. And many of them were converted and healed.

The whole affair seemed to parallel the incident in the Book of Acts when the apostles were arrested for healing the sick and casting out evil spirits. A doctor of the law, Gamaliel, stood and addressed a warning to the chief priests: "If this counsel or this work be of men, it will come to nought: But if it be of God, ye cannot overthrow it; lest haply ye be found even to fight against God" (Acts 5:38-39). Benson figured the Lord was quite capable of defending His own work, so he did exactly what the apostles had done. He "ceased not to teach and preach Jesus Christ" (Acts 5:42).

———

# 14

# A Giant Step Forward

The year 1973 was drawing to a close, and it had been a year of unprecedented progress. Through the crusades, thousands of people had accepted Christ and had been healed or delivered from evil spirits. Attendance at the Church of God Mission was now running about two thousand, and three branch churches had been opened in Benin City. More than a hundred additional branch churches throughout Nigeria were now under Benson's supervision. Numerous evangelism groups were hard at work—the Soldiers of Christ gospel team, the youth group, and several groups of Christian university students on various college campuses.

Yet Benson was unsatisfied. The fire in his bones kept him from resting on the laurels of the past, or from being content with the status quo. He was compelled to go forward, for God was directing him to take a giant step of expansion—bigger than anything they had done up to the present. He planned an end-of-year thanksgiving rally to give thanks to God for all that had been accomplished, and to present plans for the year ahead.

The night before the meeting Benson spent much time in prayer and preparation. At the Sunday rally he stood before the people and said he was appealing to them to give for the expansion of the work of God. "We need three things today," he said. "A car, an organ, and land. In a vision last night the Lord showed me a car that we are going to receive today. It is an old gray car, an Austin. The owner of this car has had it up on eight concrete blocks for the past four months. The Lord told me that the owner of that car is going to give it to us today."

A young man in the crowd, a worker with Radio Nigeria, came forward, weeping. "That is my car," he said. "I haven't been able to drive it for four months because I didn't have the money to get it fixed. But I am ready to give it."

"You are giving it to the church today to confirm what God said," Benson declared. "We will sell the car and put the money into our building program."

Next, the Nigerian police commissioner came forward and said he would give money to purchase the organ for which Benson had appealed.

The young pastor came next to his appeal for land. "We need a plot of land at least one hundred feet by one hundred feet," he said. "Or if you cannot give land, give a cash gift so that we can buy land."

At that moment a four-year-old child ran up from the crowd to the makeshift platform where his father, a lawyer, was sitting with other church and community leaders. "Daddy, Daddy, you have land," the boy said in a loud whisper which Benson could hear from where he was standing at the microphone. "Why don't you give them land?"

"Shhhh, be quiet," the man answered, taking the

child up on his lap. "Here, I'll give you a sweet. . . ." And he began searching his pockets for a piece of candy.

"No, I don't want a sweet," the boy said, shaking his head. "You have lots of land—why don't you give them land?"

Without looking behind him, Benson announced to the crowd, "God is working a miracle up here, folks!"

The man gave in. "Okay, I'll give them land," he said to his son. "Go up there and tell the pastor for me."

The little boy jumped from his father's lap and ran to Benson and tugged on his trousers. "My daddy says he will give you land," he said, so excited he could scarcely get the words out.

Benson picked up the boy, put the youngster astride his shoulders, and walked back and forth on the platform. "It has happened!" the preacher shouted. "God has given us land, and He used a child to make it happen." He explained what had just transpired between the boy and the father, and the crowd cheered with delight, then sang praises to God.

Stephen Giwa-Amu was that lawyer and at his invitation, Benson went to his office the next day to discuss details of transferring the land. It turned out he had two plots of land he was considering giving to the church, and he wanted Benson to take his choice. The pastor chose the smaller plot (250 by 510 feet) because it was on a main road, near the airport, and nearer the town than the larger plot (200 by 800 feet). Stephen Giwa-Amu also gave $1,700 at the time, and later gave a total of $20,000 for the building.

"We need your help to clear the land of brush and

rubber trees so that we can build," Benson announced to the congregation in the next service. "Please come to the site in your spare time, bring a cutlass, and help with the work." Everyone pitched in to help—elders, church leaders, missionaries, and the pastor. Benson had not forgotten from his days on the farm how to wield a cutlass, and he aptly demonstrated it.

As soon as the space where the building would stand was cleared, workers put up pegs and string to mark the perimeter of the building and began digging the trench for the foundation. One morning when Benson went out to the site, he was surprised to see all the pegs removed and the trench filled in. He was told someone connected with the city planning office had ordered it done, so Benson went to call on the man.

"You cannot build your church on that land," the official told him. "It is too close to the military hospital. We know that yours is a noisy congregation, and you will disturb the sick people nearby with your loud singing and band music."

"But it is near the airport," Benson reminded him. "And one airplane makes more noise than two hundred trumpets! God has given us that land, and we will build."

The official succeeded in suspending the work for more than a week, but he had not reckoned on the prayers of the pastor and people at the Church of God Mission. They began to pray and Benson, with the help of some businessmen in the church, began unraveling red tape until he finally had a "certificate of commencement." This he managed to acquire without the knowledge of the official who had suspended work at the building site.

Next, Benson made a trip to Lagos and got permission from the Federal Aviation Authority to build the structure thirty-five feet high, because the officials in Benin City had complained that the plans called for a building twice as high as they could allow that close to the airport.

The first trench the workers had dug had been one hundred and fifty feet long. But Benson remembered that just before he left Dallas he had paced off the Christ For The Nations headquarters building and found it was more than two hundred feet long. "If God can do that in Dallas, He can do it in Nigeria too," he said. And he gave the order to the workers to make the next trench two hundred and one feet long.

When the official who had suspended the project discovered the workers had begun digging again, he was angry. He did not yet know that Benson had acquired the necessary permits to begin. He told one of his men, "Let them go until they have the walls up about four feet high, then we'll go out there and bulldoze them down." But the man never got a chance to carry out his threat. One week later the government transferred him to another part of Nigeria, and the building program proceeded without any official interference. Today, that man is a friend of Benson's ministry.

During 1973 Benson had received the news that his teacher and mentor, Gordon Lindsay, had gone to be with the Lord. Following his unexpected death, the board of Christ For The Nations asked his wife, Freda Lindsay, to assume leadership of the organization. For

Benson, she also assumed the role of counselor and helper. He wrote and told her of the big project he was undertaking, and of his conviction that if God could do it in Dallas, He could do it in Nigeria as well. And he appealed for any financial help Christ For The Nations might be able to offer.

After the building program was well under way, Benson made a trip to the States and Mrs. Lindsay asked him to speak at Christ For The Nations. There he ministered with a powerful anointing, and challenged the people to become a part of the work of God in Nigeria. Many responded with financial help for the building costs.

A few months later, Mrs. Lindsay and some of her staff visited Benin City and saw firsthand the magnitude of the project. For years, Christ For The Nations had been helping churches overseas to complete their building programs once they were started. Through the "Native Church Foundation" founded by Gordon Lindsay, literally thousands of churches had received aid—including the Iyaro church where Benson had been ordained.

Benson's project was far bigger than the usual request for help the foundation received, but Mrs. Lindsay was challenged by the faith of Benson and the people, and the sacrifices they had made to expand the work of God. She agreed that Christ For The Nations would help put the roof on the huge building—a commitment of several thousand dollars. And there was great rejoicing among Benson's congregation.

During the time the new church was being built, news

came of an important innovation. A new television station was to be opened in Benin City, reaching all of Bendel State. (The four regions of Nigeria had now been divided into nineteen states, and Benin City is in Bendel State.) Until now, only four TV stations had existed in the entire country.

About this time, one of the leaders of the women's ministry, Deaconess Grace U. Ekperigin, had returned from a trip to Lagos with a distressing report of the immoral programs being shown on TV there. She challenged her pastor to use this powerful medium to reach people with the gospel.

The government—a military regime—owned and operated the television enterprise, using it primarily for propaganda purposes. To encourage people to buy TV sets, the government was advancing money to its workers against their salaries so they could make such a purchase.

When Benson saw how television was captivating the attention of the people, he knew it could be an effective tool. "This is the greatest opportunity for the gospel to reach this nation," he said to Margaret.

"But the station is owned by the government," his wife reminded him. "It's probably not an easy thing to get on television."

"But with God all things are possible, my dear," he replied with a smile. "And He is bigger than the government."

Benson asked Deaconess Grace to investigate the possibility of getting on television in Benin City, and to report back to him. She did not find a friendly reception.

when she explained to the program director of the TV station she was interested in buying time for a fifteen-minute weekly telecast.

"The commercial rate for a fifteen-minute segment is six hundred dollars," the director told her. "What do you want to do with this time?"

Grace replied that she was representing the Church of God Mission, and that Pastor Idahosa wanted to use the time for a Christian program.

"We cannot allow that," the woman director said, shaking her head emphatically. "This station is owned by the government. Only over my dead body will any religious programing ever be put on the air."

The messenger returned to her pastor's office weeping, and gave the negative report. But Benson was undaunted. "Don't worry," he assured her. "God will make a way, and we *will* go on that station."

He waited three weeks, then sent two other representatives to make the same inquiry from the program director. The woman was incensed by their request. "Why should we give you special consideration?" she railed at them. "The Catholics have been here for more than a hundred years, and other denominations have been around much longer than you. Church of God Mission is just a young organization that nobody ever heard of."

When that report came back, Benson was concerned. He himself went to see the woman. She kept him waiting for about twenty minutes while he seethed with indignation. She finally came into the room and the battle was joined.

"I have come to negotiate with you for television time," Benson said, rising from the chair where he had been waiting.

"Did those you sent before not give you my message?" she said curtly. "I told them, 'Only over my dead body will a gospel program go on this station.'" Unwittingly, she had made the dreadful mistake of touching God's anointed. Had she realized how seriously God views the offense, she would have trod more softly.

"No, it won't be over your dead body, madame," Benson said with conviction, shaking his head emphatically. "You will be alive, you will watch our program, and you will love it. But *you* will never be on television."

She laughed in scorn at such an outlandish statement. "It will never be so," she said. "You cannot have a religious program on this station."

"Oh, yes, it will be so," Benson said firmly. "It will be so in the name of the Lord." He walked out of her office and waited to see how God would vindicate His servant. It was almost like a contemporary rerun of Elijah's prophecy to Ahab (see 1 Kings 17:1-3).

Three months went by and nothing changed. But then there was a shake-up in the government hierarchy, and the performance of various government workers came under investigation. The woman who was program director at the television station was the first to be dismissed. She had been receiving an inflated salary for six months, and she was required to pay back the excess.

Benson heard the announcement on television, and the name was given of the man who succeeded her as program director. He was a Christian government worker who had been serving in a level-nine position, and was promoted to the level-fourteen position. Benson knew this was God's doing, and he went the very next morning to call on the man and appeal for his help.

"Jesus did something for you yesterday in allowing you to have this position," the preacher told him. "Now you have the opportunity to do something for Him."

The man agreed; he was willing to do what he could. "The problem is, this must be a commercial program," he said. "Are you prepared to pay the commercial rate prescribed by the television authority?"

"Yes, we will pay," Benson answered. "What is the rate? We want a one-hour program."

"The rate is one thousand, six hundred dollars for one hour," the man answered.

"I will be back shortly," Benson said, and he headed for the bank. There he discovered the balance in his personal account was one thousand, six hundred and four dollars. He told the banker he wanted to withdraw one thousand, six hundred dollars, and explained he was going on television to preach the gospel.

"You shouldn't do that," the banker warned. "That is too much money; it will wipe out your bank account."

"Leave four dollars in the account and give me the rest," Benson replied. He went back to the station, paid for the first telecast in advance, and scheduled the taping session.

As was the case with most projects Benson undertook, the first Redemption Hour program elicited a definite response. The denominational churches in town were jealous that such a thing was being done by what they figured to be an insignificant independent work. But the viewers over the four-state area reached by the station responded with great enthusiasm.

The TV crew taped the second program, and the director asked for the payment. "I'm waiting for a check to come, and it isn't here yet," Benson explained. The station went ahead and aired the program.

They taped the third program, and the same thing happened. In the fourth program, Benson went on the air and appealed to the viewers to help with the several thousand dollars debt they now owed the station for air time. The station authorities objected, and called Benson in to discuss it. They felt his appeal for funds was a reflection upon the station, because they had been getting letters from viewers thanking them for airing the telecast as a public service. "Why did you expose us and say you are paying?" they asked.

"But it's not free," Benson insisted. "I paid you for the first release, and I now owe you for the last three programs."

"If we reduce the price, what are you able to pay?" they asked.

"I would be pleased if you could cut the price to half—eight hundred dollars a week," Benson answered. "My members are doing everything they can to support the program with me, but this reduction would help us greatly."

By this time the station was receiving hundreds of letters from viewers who wrote and said the Redemption Hour was the best program on the station. They especially loved the singing of Benson's choir, the Redeemed

Voices, and commended the station for airing the telecast.

About four months later, Benson asked for another reduction, and the price went down to five hundred dollars a week. Over a period of eighteen months, the station continually reduced the rate until it was costing only a hundred dollars a week to air the Redemption Hour.

Progress on the new church continued through 1975, and at last it was ready for dedication. And none too soon, for the attendance was growing faster in response to the television outreach. The building was appropriately named Miracle Centre. It would house the church, the Bible school and its offices, and the headquarters office for Church of God Mission, International. The structure measured 201 by 150 by 75 feet, built at a cost of about three hundred thousand dollars—most of which was paid off by the time the church was occupied.

Dedication day was scheduled for Sunday, November 9, 1975, with the first commencement service for forty-three graduates of the Bible school to be the Saturday night before. Mrs. Gordon Lindsay was invited to be the dedication speaker, and the Rev. Chuck Flynn—who had been one of Benson's teachers at CFNI—came to speak for the commencement service.

On dedication day, Benson and the special guests arrived at the Centre almost an hour ahead of starting time to find the building was already packed to overflowing with throngs of people milling about on the outside looking for seats under the brush arbor shelters that had been erected. All told, it was probably a crowd of five or six thousand. The police band, in full uniform, sat at the entrance playing a concert for the crowd.

Ceremonies began with Mr. Giwa-Amu, the lawyer who had donated the land, cutting the ribbon stretched across the hand-carved doors at the entrance. Pastor Idahosa led the processional to the platform and the singing and rejoicing began. The foreign visitors agreed that the Nigerian Christians have a way with music that is unequaled by any other culture. They sing and praise God not just with their voices, but with every fiber of their beings. The rafters of the new building fairly shook with the reverberation of their worship.

Benson recognized the visiting dignitaries—including six government ministers and several pastors from other churches in the city—and recounted a short history of the building program. Obviously, the journalist's attempt two years earlier to destroy Benson's credibility had failed; the church had more community recognition than it ever had. And the television release had made Benson's name a household word in the community.

Mrs. Lindsay gave a message on Solomon's Temple, followed by an appeal for an offering to help reduce the remaining indebtedness. When the cash and pledges were counted, it came to more than ten thousand dollars—almost half of what was still owing on the building.

During the meeting there was an utterance in tongues, with the interpretation directed to Benson:

---

*I have given thee the forehead and the eyes of stone; nothing shall ever frighten thee. I have given thee a thick skin that no man shall destroy by evil means. Thou shalt make my voice to be heard around the world, and I shall go with thee thence. Be strong in my command and I shall increase thy armies,* says the Lord.

Following the dedication ceremonies, one hundred and seventy-six new converts were baptized in a near-by stream. That Sunday was truly a red-letter day in Benson's life, and to most observers it would seem to be the apex of his entire ministry. He had come, literally, from the oblivion of a garbage heap to a position of leadership over more than three hundred churches by the end of 1975. He was now director of a Bible school, pastor of the largest Pentecostal church in Benin City—perhaps in all of Africa—and speaker for one of the most popular TV programs in the nation. What more could a preacher ask? But in his heart Benson knew it was only a beginning.

Before leaving Benin City, Mrs. Lindsay prayed with the young pastor and as a mother in the Lord she gave him some advice: "Benson," she said earnestly, "if you stay humble before God, giving Him all the glory, and keep up your prayer life and study of the Word, the whole world will hear of your faith and your exploits."

# 15

# A God of Multiplication

The television outreach soon expanded to other parts of Nigeria, and a few nearby countries began to be reached by either radio or television—Ghana, Togo, Dahomey, and Cameroon. The potential listening and viewing audience surpassed fifty million people, and letters of response began pouring into the Miracle Centre office. Benson began publishing *Redemption Faith* magazine four times a year, as well as distributing Bibles and Christian books to those who requested them. Invitations came for him to go to other African countries for crusades.

As the ministry continued to grow, Benson knew the financial base also had to expand. But experience had taught him not to hold back for lack of funds; if he walked in faith, the need would be met.

He had always taught his people to give, but after his return from Dallas he emphasized it more forcefully. In a nation where much of the population finds it difficult to scrape together enough food to stay alive, not many preachers deliver sermons on giving, but Benson did. A favorite text was Prov. 11:24: "There is that scattereth, and yet increaseth, and there is that witholdeth more than is meet, but it tendeth to poverty."

"When you scatter by giving this year, it shall yield return and multiply," he told his people. "But if you withhold it, it will tend you to poverty. Therefore scatter and it shall increase, for multiplication brings the glory of God. If you identify your money with His own money, God will multiply it for you. If you give Him your time, He will increase your years; if you give Him your life, He will give you a renewed life; if you give Him any kind of gift, it shall bring forth fruit of its own kind. No one ever beats God at giving. He is a God of multiplication. When you give anything to God, he returns it to you in abundance. There is no shortage in God. I rejoice today that while I gave God one life—one body, one spirit, one soul—thousands upon thousands have been multiplied."

The people responded and began to give. They gave for the building project, for the television outreach, for evangelistic crusades, for literature production, and for the needs of their pastors. Financial help also came from other partners, but the people of Miracle Centre Church of God Mission gave sacrificially. And the law of sowing and reaping worked, just as their pastor promised it would.

When the land on which Miracle Centre was built was first acquired, only one family in the congregation owned a car—a Volkswagen. Because the building site was several miles from the city center, many of the people had to take taxis or walk long distances in order to help with the volunteer work on the building. But gradually, prosperity testimonies began coming in— about a man being promoted on his job, another receiving a salary increase, an unemployed person finding a job, or a farmer being blessed with an abundant harvest. The more the people gave, the more the blessings rained upon them.

By the time the Miracle Centre was dedicated in 1975, dozens of cars were parked around the building. Within two or three years, a uniformed traffic officer was put on duty every Sunday to direct traffic. Several parking lot attendants were assigned to help organize the parking of literally hundreds of cars and motor-cycles, and additional space for parking had to be provided. It was a common occurrence for the church leaders to conduct a special service for the dedication of another group of brand-new cars with which some of the members had been blessed.

Increasing numbers of crusades were conducted in various parts of Nigeria, which meant new branch churches of the Church of God Mission continued to proliferate. In 1975 alone, more than one hundred churches were opened. Rev. S.G. Elton, Benson's primary advisor, helped to oversee the crusade follow-up efforts. He wrote in his report dated March 15, 1976:

> We are fully committed to seeing that every soul who confesses the Lord Jesus as Saviour and Lord is also contacted again by a church leader or member and made to understand that it is only by continuing in the faith and growing in grace of the Lord Jesus that he can grow spiritually. This task is not as spectacular as the crusades, but just as essential and important, and we have a large force

of young people who have been trained for this task.

In the recent crusades in Calabar and Uyo the estimated number of converts runs into thousands, and they came from many different towns and villages. We managed to secure the names and addresses of many of them and they are being contacted and sent literature. Also, suitable classes for converts are being arranged in each village or town where we can send a trained Christian.

Another area of outreach that continued to grow was the work among university students all over Nigeria. Groups of Christian students as large as four hundred or more were meeting regularly for study and teaching on the campuses in Benin City, Ibadan, Ife, and Zaria. On weekends they "attacked" prisons, boarding schools, schools, and hospitals with the gospel, with impressive results. Missionary Elton wrote in a June, 1977 report of another unique method of evangelism:

The final year students are busy with their final exams, and as they complete their academic work they have to go out for ten months national service in remote and neglected areas chosen by the federal government. This has been the government plan for some years now, and we eagerly fit into it because the Christian students hope they will be sent to the Moslem north where they can witness and preach Jesus Christ. Thus the federal government is actually paying for these young people to take the gospel into the areas sealed from missionary work. They have done a wonderful job in past years, and this is proved by the many complaints received from the Moslem leaders against the federal government for sending Christians into their areas. But no one can forbid the Christians from witnessing and meeting with others in their own houses and residences.

This year we laid hands on and sent out a large number—more than one hundred and twenty at Ife University, nearly two hundred in Ibadan, and large numbers in other universities as well. During university vacations there are hundreds of groups of young people gathering for schools of evangelism to train in the work of the Lord. We estimate there at least fifty thousand young people in camps for this purpose right now. We keep in touch with them all by mail and regular newsletters, magazines and books.

Inevitably, as large numbers of young people became involved in evangelism, many of them chose to train for full-time ministry. While the Miracle Centre building provided classroom and office space for the Bible school, dormitory space was urgently needed. So another building project soon got under way. Meanwhile, many students were so eager to secure training that they slept on the floor of the Miracle Centre while waiting for the dormitories to be completed.

When Benson went to other African countries for crusades, he always offered scholarships to a few key young people from those countries to come to Benin City for training. He raised funds to cover their boarding costs, then sent these scholarship students back to their home territories to evangelize and build churches. Crusades were held—and students signed up—in Mombasa and Nairobi, Kenya; Accra, Tema, and Kumasi in Ghana; Lome, Togo; Monrovia, Liberia; and Kinshasa, Zaire.

At first the school was named Christ For Nigeria Bible Institute, but soon the name had to be changed to allow for a broader scope. Benson chose the new name: All Nations For Christ Bible Institute.

The All Nations For Christ Bible School is presently working towards a higher academic level. Transcripts for those desiring a B.A. degree will be submitted to I.C.I. for accreditation. This is the first school.

The second school is SEED—Seminary of Extensive Education Development. The SEED School is in two parts. SEED I is designed to train further those pastors already in the field. SEED II is for those working towards a B.A. degree through I.C.I. in Brussels.

The third school is The School of French Studies. God is opening the door for us to train many young men and women from French-speaking countries. We are also encouraging the government to send students to our school for training instead of sending them to another country.

One of the problems we have faced when we send students from African countries to other countries to study is that many of them decide to remain in that country and not return to Africa. Therefore, we have wasted time, money and lost valuable resources. Because of this, we are believing God to allow us to have the staff, expertise, finances, methods, ways and means to teach and train Africans in Nigeria who will teach and train others. We are believing God to give us qualified and professional teachers who will conduct the same courses which an African would receive by studying in England or the United States or some other country.

The ministry was growing so fast that Benson obviously could not do on his own everything that needed to be done. One of the elders who had worked with Benson for several years—J.B.S. Coker—had been ordained as a local pastor in Benin City, and he led the ministry of Miracle Centre while Benson was away with the crusade team. Other elders helped in various areas of leadership, such as oversight of the dormitory construction, or directing the Redeemed Voices choir. Additional missionaries were recruited to help with the teaching and administrative load of the Bible school, and Benson scheduled his taping sessions for the television program around his traveling schedule. But no matter how busy he was, he made a point of having a meeting with Brother Elton once each month to keep him informed, and to seek his counsel.

At times Benson felt the load of it all was more than he could manage. Then he would recall the vision the Lord had given him, and think of the millions still carrying a load of sin who needed to hear that Jesus could set them free. He wondered if the tree in the vision—which he had seen expanding to provide

---

shelter for more and more people—was going to stretch out to cover all of Africa and the world at large!

But he believed that as God multiplied the work, He would also multiply the workers and the finances necessary to sustain it. "I must never forget that my name means 'attentive to God,' " he thought. "As long as God keeps speaking to me and I keep listening, we will be victorious!"

# 16

# A Fiery Furnace

Three areas of ministry now required more of Benson's time and energy than any others: the television outreach, the evangelistic crusades, and the constant building program for the Bible school. Each of them, to carry on, needed large amounts of money. Though the people of Church of God Mission International were giving sacrificially, and the number of constituents was steadily increasing, Benson knew he needed additional support to keep the program going.

An American missionary working in another part of Africa had observed Benson's ministry and recognized his potential for helping with evangelism efforts in other nations on the continent. He suggested that Benson and Margaret accompany him to the States where they could visit churches to raise funds for a series of crusades in various African countries.

The three of them set out on the itinerary arranged by the missionary, and everywhere they went people responded to Benson's ministry with great enthusiasm. He met pastors and church leaders who were awakened to the need for evangelism in Africa, and financial help began coming in for the crusades.

During that 1976 tour of the United States, an

American evangelist heard about Benson's ministry and recommended him to Jim Bakker of the PTL television network, which had been on the air for a relatively short time. PTL paid expenses for Benson and the missionary to fly to Charlotte, North Carolina, for an appearance on Jim Bakker's talk show.

But when they arrived at the studio the duo heard disappointing news. "I'm sorry, but because of scheduling problems, you'll only be able to be on the show for five minutes," the PTL representative explained. The missionary was upset; all their arrangements to get there seemed a wasted effort. But Benson resolved to make the most of the time available on the air, and waited patiently until they were summoned to the set where the program was already underway before a live audience.

The moment he had an opportunity to speak, Benson shared how the Lord had helped them to get on television in Nigeria when everyone had said it was impossible. Jim Bakker's interest perked up. "This is the greatest opportunity we have ever had to reach the millions in Nigeria with the gospel," Benson declared. "And I am ready to make my program and its time available to you for your first overseas PTL release."

During the live broadcast, Jim Bakker said, "Beginning today, PTL will take over that program in Africa." The studio audience cheered and praised the Lord.

Benson briefly related a few more facts about the ministry in Nigeria, and the time was gone. It had been a short encounter indeed, but those five minutes proved to be life-changing ones for Benson. PTL immediately assumed the responsibility of paying for television air time in Nigeria, and Benson renamed the program "PTL Redemption Hour." He left North Carolina with the conviction that this was just the first of many visits to the "PTL Club." And he was right.

To Benson, one of the greatest miracles in his ministry is the way God brought him into contact with Jim Bakker of "PTL Club." It cannot be explained on the level of human understanding. Only God knows the millions of lives reached through this end-time media of soul-winning—reached for Christ in their own living rooms, prison cells, hospital rooms and in convention halls.

Even in areas where there is no electricity, there are television sets. The government supplies all of its secondary schools with generators of electricity on school grounds. They also provide each school with a television set. What an opportunity to reach the future leaders of the nation with the gospel.

The television outreach is one of the most exciting ministries in Africa today. Benson gives all of the glory for the television ministry to God and he is especially thankful for the Rev. and Mrs. Jim Bakker and the PTL partners for their love and concern.

Benson and Margaret and the missionary moved on to meetings booked in Canada, but back in Nigeria serious trouble was brewing. The young preacher had discovered early in his ministry that the strongest opposition to the work of evangelism usually did not come from unbelievers, but from other religious groups. This also proved to be true concerning complaints about the television program.

Several religious organizations in Benin City were irate because Benson's gospel program was on the air. But one group got together enough money to try to do something about it. A representative of that group offered a bribe to the station's commercial controller to take Benson off the air. The former controller who had helped Benson to acquire air time in the beginning had been transferred, and someone else now held the position. The new man told the rival group's representative that to get Benson's time slot they would have to pay one thousand, two hundred dollars a week—a greal deal more than Benson was paying.

As it happened, a worker at the station who was sympathetic to Benson's ministry discovered the attempt to sabotage the "Redemption Hour" program. He went to Pastor Coker at the Miracle Centre office with this information. The commercial controller at the TV station—who knew Benson was out of the country—had addressed a letter to Benson giving seven days notice that he would have to pay the new rate of one thousand, two hundred dollars a week for the telecast, or be taken off the air. But the plan was to withhold the letter for six days and only submit it the day before the deadline, apparently assuming that with Benson out of the country, and with only one day's notice, the staff would be powerless to do anything about the situation.

The worker who had discovered the plot was a contributor to Benson's ministry. He donated money for a round-trip ticket to New York so that a Miracle Centre staff member could go to the States to find Benson and bring him home to handle the matter.

Meanwhile, Pastor Coker told some of the church leaders what was happening, and they began to pray.

The Church of God Mission staff member got to New York to discover that Benson was in Canada. He finally got through by telephone and told Benson there was an emergency at home; he must return to Nigeria at once. Benson and Margaret were frightened. Their first thought was that perhaps something was wrong with the children; yet they felt confident that God would protect their little ones. Benson canceled his meeting, left Margaret in the care of the missionary with whom they were traveling, and flew that same day to New York.

He met the staff member at JFK Airport, read the information concerning the TV station's action, and realized he must act at once. He managed to get a flight that same night to Lagos, arriving the next morning in time to get an immediate connection to Benin City. He went straight from the airport to the office of the governor of Nigeria's Bendel State to protest. Little more than forty-eight hours had transpired since the office worker had discovered the plot.

"Reverend Idahosa!" the governor exclaimed, obviously surprised to see him. "You told me just three weeks ago that you would be away for three months; why are you back so soon?"

"Someone has sabotaged our program and is trying to take us off the air," Benson said. "My staff got word to me of what was happening, and I have come back to ask you to intervene in the situation."

The governor confronted the station manager, who

insisted that if Benson wanted to stay on the air he would have to pay the new rate of one thousand, two hundred dollars a week. "The government does not provide sufficient funds for us to operate the station," he explained. "We have to sell time to those who are willing to pay the commerical rate, and this other group has agreed to do that."

Benson pointed out that the other group had assets from various business enterprises, while he relied upon donations to pay for the time. He asked for special consideration, and the manager agreed to allow a 15 percent discount off the commercial rate—which meant the total fee would be nine hundred dollars a week. That figure was still much higher than Benson had been paying, but he agreed, confident the Lord would provide.

"You can resume your tour of the States," the governor told him; "this problem is taken care of." The program missed only two Sundays, and then was back on the air.

Benson returned to the States and presented the situation to Jim Bakker, who agreed that PTL would pay the nine hundred dollars a week the station demanded. When the dust finally settled, instead of losing the Benin station as his enemies had planned, the broadcast expanded—with the help of PTL—to include the station at Ibadan, which reached viewers not only in the capital city of Lagos, but also in the Muslim territories to the north.

It became increasingly evident to the young preacher that the expanding outreach of his ministry was truly beyond his own ability, and beyond the power of the enemy to stop it. God had placed His sovereign stamp of blessing upon it, and continued miraculously to provide the resources for sustaining it.

Benson returned from his stateside tour and began the planning and preparation for mass crusades in other nations of Africa. Despite the misunderstanding of those with a smaller vision, or those who questioned the different ways God used each individual, Benson like Abraham of old, continued to walk by faith, following the leading of God to fulfill the call of God upon his life. His horizon now reached beyond his province, beyond his country, even beyond his continent. He would be heard in the world because God had found a willing vessel, one whose heart and spirit cried, "Lord, here am I, use me." And the fire in his bones burned even more intensely.

# 17

# Reaping a Harvest

A typical crusade was the one held in Kinshasa, Zaire, in May, 1978. The evangelist's wife, Margaret Idahosa, who often accompanied him in the crusades, wrote a complete report of the Kinshasa crusade for the *Redemption Faith* magazine. The following are some excerpts from that report:

" 'Jesus the same yesterday, today and forever' was prominently inscribed on the crusade banner that hung above the platform and welcomed all to the service at Kasavubu Square in Kinshasa. A steady flow of many types of people continued all through the service. Different denominations were represented—Catholic, Baptist, Presbyterian, Pentecostal, and a host of other denominations—showing how God's Spirit is being poured out 'on all flesh' (Joel 2:28).

"One could sense a strong feeling of expectation and anticipation before the service began at 3:00 P.M. The fixed time of the meeting was quite unusual as I had never attended an afternoon crusade.

"At precisely 3:30 P.M., Reverend B.A. Idahosa arrived at the crusade grounds. We were later informed that as early as 1:30 P.M., men and women defied the scorching sun and abandoned their various activities to rush down to the Square.

"Mounting the platform, blistering with the fervor of the Holy Ghost, Reverend Idahosa opened his mouth to declare the hidden mysteries of God's Word. He took his text from Malachi 3:6, 'I am the Lord, I change not.'

"The message was a package of God's power and blessings, so much so that about one thousand persons trooped forward for prayers in response to the altar call to receive Christ into their lives. After the salvation prayer, Rev. Idahosa called to the platform two members of the audience, a man and a woman, who were both deaf. They were prayed for and both of them felt the Master's touch and were healed.

"Afterwards a general prayer was said for the sick. Testimonies of diverse kinds of outstanding miracles took place. In all, three lame walked, six blind had their sight restored, others who complained of stomach and chest pains and acute headaches were healed. The sound of their voices shouting for joy rent the air.

"Of all the miracles that took place in the first night, I shall not forget the incident of a blind boy who came to the meeting. He heard the message of redemption and received the Lord Jesus into his heart. When prayers for the sick were said, even though others received healing, this lad was not healed of his blindness. But miraculously, on his way home after the close of the meeting, suddenly his blind eyes were opened.

"The lad was so excited by it all that he did not know what to do other than to dash quickly to one of the elders in the Bishop's church to testify how the Lord's healing virtue reached him."

## Second Night

"As early as 11:00 A.M. news was reaching us at our hotel lounge that people had started going to the crusade grounds. Before our arrival the Square was already filled to capacity. When we mounted the platform and looked down upon the excited crowd who held their hands up high rejoicing, the sight of their lovely palms reminded me of a ripe wheat field ready for harvest.

"The crowd was so compacted that the heat emitted by their breath was felt by each one of us on the platform as that of an exposed oven. I saw in them a real hunger for the Word of God, so much so that whatever you had asked them to do would have been joyfully done without question.

"Rev. Idahosa came out to preach the gospel of Jesus with power. He made the people understand that the devil had never made anything good, neither will he do so. Rather, the devil is a killer, destroyer, thief, and an intruder. A hater of God and His people, a liar who roars about like a lion seeking whom he may devour. He made them understand that the devil is not the Lion. He emphasized that the devil only roars *like* a lion but that he is not the Lion. There is only one Lion: He is from the Tribe of Judah, and His name is Jesus Christ, who bore our griefs and carried away our sorrows and by whose stripes we were healed. He also told them that the devil is the root cause of all sicknesses.

"He exhorted that the only answer to these problems is in the blood of Jesus, and that if they give their lives to Him as a seed, healing—which is the children's bread—will be theirs.

"At the end of the message he made an altar call and about two thousand people responded to give their lives to Jesus. Prayers were said for them, following which he asked the crowd to throw their rings, charms, amulets, cigarettes and match boxes to the platform in order to offer a general deliverance prayer. They obeyed. While some threw their various demonic trinkets toward the stage, others threw them directly at him. He assured them not to bother about him, that he was totally immune to the influence of the charms as he was covered in the blood of Jesus. This exercise lasted for about twenty minutes.

"Rev. Idahosa then opened his mouth and commanded the healing wind of Jesus to touch and heal all that were sick. As he was ending his prayer, miracles started happening. The lame jumped up, the deaf heard, the blind received sight, the dumb spoke; many that were afflicted by different kinds of ailments were healed.

"In that night alone, I witnessed four lame walking, jumping and leaping up as their joy knew no bounds. In addition, six blind saw, five deaf and mute spoke and had their hearing restored! Other healings that took place that night included epilepsy, stomach pain and chest pain. Those healed frantically pushed forward to the platform to testify of what God had done for them.

"I will not forget a lady who came jumping for joy to testify that she had been hospitalized for a long period while she was operated upon three times, but her case did not improve. She confessed that when the man of God prayed she felt as if someone touched her stomach and all of a sudden her tumor disappeared!"

*Third Night*

"The servant of God came out to minister as before, but when he opened his Bible to preach, the Spirit of God told him to call on a lame man who was in great pain and sat in front of the platform. So he called the man to the stage for prayer. He immediately told all the lame on the floor and those with crutches and walking sticks to raise them up to God, which they did. He prayed a short prayer and the Lord had compassion on them. When the prayer was over, cripples threw away their crutches and other walking aids, and ran to the platform to testify of the miracle the Lord performed on them. There were twenty-two lame people who walked—nine of them children whose ages were between three and eight years. Prayer was said only for the lame, but the blind received sight, the dumb spoke, and the deaf heard.

"There was a great confusion in the crowd as they pushed and pressed to the platform to testify. This took about thirty minutes before the minister was able to get them organized for the message.

"As soon as he opened his Bible, miracles started happening again. The crowd was divided into groups of people. When miracles started happening at all the sides of the crusade ground, there were shouts of joy and praises to God saying, 'he's seeing,' 'he's speaking,' 'he's walking,' 'she's talking!' The power of God was moving like a whirlwind on the field from one end of the Square to the other, and the man of God did not stop it from moving. All he did was to magnify, praise and bless the Almighty King of Kings, Lord of Lords, the great Alpha and Omega, GOD who liveth and reigneth forever and ever.

"The testimonies were so many that the man of God was left with no time to preach any more that night. It became dark, and people had to catch the bus to go to their homes, for many came from far and near. Rev. Idahosa told the crowd to go home and requested them to come to one of the Pentecostal churches in Kinshasa the next day, which was Sunday. On that Sunday the pastor told us that people started coming to the service as early as 6:00 A.M. When we got to the church at about 8:45 A.M., the crowd outside was more than the crowd inside the hall. When we saw the zeal in their faces and actions, we were moved with compassion in our hearts.

"Rev. Idahosa preached the sermon on 'Prosperity.' He made the people realize that God is interested in their prosperity as well as in their souls; he said Christians were expected to be the head and not the tail. At the service were top government dignitaries, traditional chiefs, court judges, and military personnel who listened admirably and took down points as the minister preached."

*The Crowning Night*
"At about 3:00 P.M., the crusade grounds were

---

packed full with people thristy for the living Word of God. Rev. Idahosa came with a song, *'Asante Sana Yesu'* (meaning 'Thank you, thank you, Jesus' in Swahili).

"He turned to his text in Mark 10:46-52 about blind Bartimaeus who cried out, 'Jesus, thou Son of David, have mercy on me!' The devil, the pushing crowd, and the spectators asked him to hold his peace, but the Scripture says he shouted the more. The minister told the crowd that Jesus understands every situation, pain, heartache, vision, problem and every heart cry, but He will require them to channel these problems to Him with their lips.

"Rev. Idahosa thereby encouraged and built their faith. At this juncture, he requested them to ask God for their needs and hearts' desires just as Bartimaeus asked, without listening to the dissenting voice of the enemy. The crowd's prayer, and the sound of their voices sounded like the falling rain. They prayed out their hearts to God. Then the reverend prayed a compassionate prayer for them all. After that he sang a song, 'There's Power in the Blood of Jesus,' and asked them to examine their bodies and run to the platform to testify of what the Lord had done for them. By the time the chorus was sung three times, the platform was packed full with people healed of diverse kinds of ailments; we had to move the chairs to make room for people to stand to testify.

"I will never forget the woman who had had a body cast from her chest to her waist for one year, whom the Lord healed miraculously. She came rejoicing to say that for the past year she had been in bed, six months in the hospital and six months at home, never sitting but all the time lying on her back. 'And now the Lord has healed me without any cost and I am free!' she shouted. The cast was cut off her body with a knife.

Another woman came to testify that for seven years she had been lame, but now God had healed her. She could not contain herself with the joy and she burst into tears telling people, 'I am walking again!'

"Many people left their walking sticks, crutches, and hearing aids at the platform for a testimony to the glory of God. Another exciting miracle was the heap of cigarettes and different kinds of charms the people threw to the platform as a sign of total surrender to the Lord Jesus."

*Highlights*

"In spite of the tense political atmosphere in Shaba Province in Zaire, the government gave full cooperation for the crusade. One would have thought that as there was war in a particular area of the country, all forms of gathering should have been discouraged, let alone a crowded crusade meeting of about ninety thousand people. Thank God, the government realized the answer to social and political problems is from God.

"Two government planes hovered around the crusade grounds from the first day to the last to ensure that nobody disturbed the meetings. When some top government officials heard what God was doing in Kinshasa, they delegated a government official to the crusade to ask for prayers for the war to end. This Reverend Idahosa did.

"Four flags of different countries were flown high to represent the countries that were present at the Kinshasa meeting. Free scholarships were given to four Zairians to study the Word of God at the Bible school in Benin City."

Each crusade was memorable for one reason or another, and the miracles God performed to make the crusades possible at all were legion. In Monrovia, Liberia, the difficulty was to get the local churches to be involved in the planning of the crusade. A Christian broadcasting corporation there refused to make broadcasts announcing the crusade program because the advertising posters for the meeting claimed that God would heal the sick during the crusade. The preplanning work was finally done by a group of Christian students at the University of Liberia, and the local Lutheran bishop cooperated with the crusade effort. He later testified, "Of all the crusades I have attended, and of all the radio messages I have listened to, this crusade has done the most for my life as an individual."

In Kumasi, Ghana, bureaucratic red tape threatened to hinder the crusade, but when Benson appealed to the Regional Commissioner for cooperation, the man consented. In the end, the government actually provided the platform, loud speakers, a lighting system, and two sound-equipped vehicles for making announcements of the crusade at Jackson Park. Another highlight of that meeting came when the King of Ashanti, his wife, and some of his chiefs attended the crusade. Following Benson's salvation message, the king and his wife stood with hands raised to God as a sign of surrender to Him. Some of the chiefs who came with the king stood also.

In Accra, Ghana, the people were particularly responsive to Benson's ministry because they were already familiar with the Redemption Hour television program which was being aired there. An astonishing miracle was instrumental in gaining the attention of the media and of the government officials.

One afternoon a construction worker fell from the top of the tall building on which he was working, and crashed to the sidewalk many stories below. As it happened, he fell only a few feet from the spot where Benson was standing. The pedestrians in the area assumed the man must certainly be dead after falling such a distance, and they all fled in fear. Blood was gushing from the man's eyes, ears, nose and mouth, and he was unconscious. Benson knelt beside him, lifted him up, and began to pray, claiming the power of God to heal the man. Soon the man stirred, regained consciousness, and began to speak. By this time his co-workers who had also been working at the top of the new building arrived on the scene, and were astonished when they found their comrade alive. Benson placed the man in the care of the workers and went on to his quarters.

The event caused no small stir in the city, and word of it reached the Ghanian Head of State, who received Benson at the State House to thank him for bringing the crusade to his country. Before the meetings concluded, attendance was estimated at one hundred twenty thousand people. One of the sponsoring pastors said, "The Ghana crusade was a spiritual earthquake. Miracles upon miracles happened. Ghana has never had it so great—not even with Rev. Billy Graham. This is the first of its kind."

The Nairobi, Kenya, crusade was most outstanding because of the record-breaking crowds attending the meetings. On the final day, a veritable sea of humanity flowed onto the crusade grounds. Local authorities estimated the crowd as being between one hundred fifty thousand and two hundred thousand people; it was impossible to estimate the number of people who accepted Christ or were healed.

Despite the threat of rebellion and gunfire, the crusade in Kampala, Uganda, touched the lives of thousands of people in that war-torn country. Night meetings were not allowed because of the fighting, so thousands gathered in the blistering early afternoon sun to hear Benson's messages. Working people could not attend the midday meetings, but live coverage was provided on radio, reaching additional thousands of people.

Soldiers and policemen, on duty to keep order in the crowd, wept their way to repentance, along with hundreds of others who accepted Christ as their Savior. Innumerable miracles of healing occurred during the five days. In a TV interview Benson spoke to the entire nation, encouraging the people of Uganda to believe in themselves and their country, and to serve both by forgiving, forgetting the past, and having faith in God. Following the crusade, the government ministry of information offered Benson free time to air the "PTL

Redemption Hour" on both the television and radio government stations.

The crusades also reached beyond Africa—to Stockholm, Jonkoping, and Goteborg, Sweden; Singapore, Kuala Lumpur, and Penang, Malaysia; Busan and Seoul, Korea; the United States; and Canberra, Australia.

Benson was invited to Australia in 1980 for a nationwide crusade. Rev. Harry Westcott hosted this crusade. The host reports that as a result of the crusade, he now has a new vision for Australia. He acknowledges that Benson's ministry is responsible for enlightening him and giving him the vision and thrust for his present ministry. Rev. Westcott is the PTL host for the nations of Australia.

God sent Benson to Trinidad to assist a young ministry that needed strengthening. As a result of what God did, the work in Trinidad is growing rapidly and God has given new vision to the workers there.

He was invited as the keynote speaker to Impetus 80 in Sri Lanka (formerly Ceylon). The purpose of Impetus 80 was to bring Christian leaders of the Third World together in order to challenge them and to encourage them to go in faith to implement a plan to bring revival to their nations. Over thirty-nine nations were represented at this convention in Sri Lanka, including India, the Philippines, Greece, Kenya, Uganda, Ghana, Togo, Ivory Coast, Liberia, Cameroon, Zaire, Egypt, Turkey, Singapore, and many others.

As a result of Impetus 80, Benson is now receiving

letters from many of the leaders from other nations for him to come to their countries to hold meetings and crusades and to further challenge and teach them. He presently is scheduled to hold crusades in 1982 in India, Greece, Tanzania and Zimbabwe. He will travel to Korea in 1983 for a crusade.

In 1968 when the Lord had spoken to Benson and told him, *"I have called you that you might take the gospel around the world in my name,"* the young preacher could not truly comprehend the scope of that calling. Now, almost ten years later, the call was being fulfilled. Benson was doing what God had asked him to do: *"Preach the gospel. . . ."* And it was abundantly evident that God was keeping His end of the bargain: *"I will confirm my Word with signs following."*

# 18

# The Women Too

The scope and outreach of Benson's ministry went through a veritable explosion. It seemed apparent that Gordon Lindsay's prayer for God to pour a double portion of power upon this young man's ministry was being answered. But the mantle that fell on his shoulders also touched the shoulders of the helpmeet who stood beside him.

Margaret enjoyed her role as a mother and a pastor's wife, despite her earlier protests that she did not want to marry a preacher. She kept things running smoothly at home, and helped keep Benson on an even keel. But she was also developing strong leadership qualities of her own. She often prayed and counseled with people, she sometimes served as an interviewer and reporter in the crusades, and she continued to teach part time at a local government school.

After the birth of her son "Feb," Margaret found that her mother, who still practiced juju worship, was much more open to the gospel. She had seen the faithfulness of God in her daughter's life when her grandson was born, and she could not deny the miracles she had witnessed through her son-in-law's ministry. At last Margaret convinced her to pray the sinner's prayer and receive

Christ as her Savior. Then they had a great celebration when the idol of Olokun and all the paraphernalia she used for juju rites were burned in a bonfire. A heavy weight was lifted off Margaret's heart when she felt the assurance that her mother was now a believer.

When "Feb" was several months old, Margaret learned that another baby was on the way. And about the same time she had the opportunity to go to England to take a course of studies in home economics at Huddersfield Polytechnic College. She went with Benson's blessing. She lived with a friend in Leeds who helped take care of the baby while she attended classes at the college several miles away. While still in England, she gave birth to Ruth Eloghosa Benson Idahosa on March 8, 1974.

Margaret not only learned all she could in the home economics course, but she also visited churches in the area and observed their education programs, their child evangelism efforts, etc. Before returning to Nigeria she attended a church convention where ideas were presented for various aspects of outreach for the local church. She was particularly impressed with what she observed in women's ministries in that convention. She heard speakers tell of programs for women's Bible studies, practical studies in marriage helps and child rearing, sewing, and home decorating. She took careful notes on everything and asked many questions.

Back in Benin City, she studied her notes and asked God to help her adapt what could be used in Nigeria, and establish a women's ministry at the Church of God Mission. With Benson's encouragement she called a meeting of all the women in the community and shared a Bible study with them, and related what she had learned about women's ministries in England. The women responded with enthusiasm, and wanted to have their own meeting one evening a week. Margaret taught Bible studies for the meetings, and called on others to speak to the women on other subjects.

Then Evangelist and Mrs. T.L. Osborn came to Benin City for a crusade, for which Benson was the co-ordinator. After the crusade, Margaret shared with Daisy Osborn her desire to organize a ministry for women. Mrs. Osborn encouraged Margaret to move ahead, and volunteered to speak to the women herself before she and her husband left Nigeria. The special meeting was announced, and hundreds of women packed into the Iyaro church.

"Don't be content to walk behind your husbands," Mrs. Osborn told them. "Stand beside them in the ministry of the church and be a part of what God is doing. You can have a great impact upon your husbands, your children and families, and the community." At the conclusion of her message she led the women in a prayer of dedication to become involved in a special ministry for women. That was the beginning of the Christian Women's Fellowship, International, with Margaret Idahosa as founding president.

In 1976 Margaret and the leaders of the new fellowship scheduled their first Women's Convention and invited women from the Church of God Mission congregations all over Nigeria. Daisy Osborn came from the States to be the main speaker, and she challenged the hundreds of delegates attending the conference to establish a women's center that would minister to the local community and then reach out to the entire nation. She led the group in a united prayer that God would provide the land and the funds for such a center to be built. Mrs. Osborn also agreed to serve as advisor for the Christian Women's Fellowship, International.

When the conference was over, Mr. Stephen Giwa-Amu donated a large plot of land on which the center would be built. Margaret and her committee spent many hours drawing up detailed plans for the development of the project. They finally settled on an eight-unit plan:

*Unit One:* An auditorium to seat three thousand women to be used for special women's meetings and conferences. Mothers and singles from all over Africa will be invited to attend seminars and conventions to learn child care, home economics, nutrition, nursing, prenatal care and other areas pertaining to the care of the entire family.

*Unit Two:* Guest facilities to provide housing for out-of-town guests coming to Benin City for conferences.

*Unit Three:* The evangelism unit, where women will be trained as "gospel ambassadors" to go out into the government schools and teach the Bible and Christian principles as a part of the school curriculum. Government school leaders have already agreed to cooperate with this program. The women, after receiving evangelism training, would also go into hospitals, rest homes, and prisons to witness and teach the Bible.

*Unit Four:* The day-care unit, providing a place where working mothers can leave their children from the age of six weeks to be cared for in a Christian atmosphere. Because of the rapid rate of inflation, increasing numbers of Nigerian women are being forced to get jobs in order to support their families, and child-care facilities are almost nonexistent. The Women's Center will offer this service for a modest fee, and also provide a health and child-care clinic as a part of the program. Doctors, nurses and midwives will teach child-care sessions for the mothers, and women will also be trained to go out into the villages and rural areas to conduct such training sessions.

*Unit Five:* The Christian day-school unit, which will be an educational program for children from kindergarten through grade ten. The standard curriculum used in government schools will be implemented, but the Bible will be included as a study unit so that the Christian faith is a part of the child's learning experience from an early age. Working with the children will provide opportunities to reach the parents and entire families with the gospel message.

*Unit Six:* The orphanage unit will provide a place where unfortunate and abandoned children can be cared for and educated. Dormitories will house them, Christian houseparents will nurture them, and they will be enrolled in the Christian school program.

*Unit Seven:* The home economics unit will offer training for women in every aspect of homemaking: cooking, cleaning, child care, nutrition, home decoration, sewing, laundry methods, and spiritual training of their children. This unit will also train women who will go to the villages and rural areas to teach these skills.

*Unit Eight:* The gymnasium unit will be a place where physical fitness will be taught to the women as well as to the children enrolled in the Christian school. It will also be used for athletic events and other activities.

The six-million-dollar project is to be developed over

a period of several years. In March, 1979, the ground-breaking ceremony for the first building was held and several thousand dollars were contributed by those who attended. In October, 1980, the child-care program—Unit Four—began operation. The Africa for Christ, Inc., Washington, D.C. assisted Rev. Idahosa in recruiting two American Missionaries to teach in Nigeria. They have established a Day Care/Primary School under CWFI's direction. Within two months more than eighty students were enrolled. Already Margaret is receiving requests from women of other nations in Africa who want her help in establishing a program for ministry to women in their areas.

Eventually the responsibility of helping her husband in the ministry, caring for her family, and directing the women's ministry kept Margaret so occupied that she gave up her teaching job. By this time she had two more little girls: Daisy Osagumwenro Margaret born May 12, 1975, and Freda Deonne Ehimuenma born April 22, 1979. Little Freda was the first baby to be enrolled in the day-care program, so her mother could continue directing the program and raising funds for future development of the Women's Center.

Of the helpmeet the Lord gave him, Benson can truly say with the ancient writer: "A wife of noble character who can find? She is worth far more than rubies. Her husband has full confidence in her and lacks nothing of value. She brings him good, not harm, all the days of her life" (Prov. 31:10-12, NIV).

# 19

# God's Bright Promises

Evangelism—first, last and always—was and continues to be the nerve center of Benson's ministry. The greater the results of the evangelism outreach, the more he realized the importance of follow-up. All those converts needed teaching; the new churches being established needed pastors; those being called to full-time ministry needed training; more workers were needed to extend the evangelism and follow-up efforts. But he had long ago learned not to concentrate on the problem, rather to move full steam ahead with the solution.

Benson's greatest problem in the ministry had always been coping with people who said of each new venture, "It cannot be done." He had been told it would be impossible to found a new church in Benin City. Now there are fifteen Church of God Mission congregations there, plus more than six hundred and fifty similar churches in Nigeria and nine other countries.

He had been told he and Margaret could never have children. The Lord has given them four, when they asked for only three!

He had been told, "You cannot go on television in Nigeria." Now he directs the largest Christian TV outreach in Africa.

The critics said, "You can't reach all of Nigeria—especially the Muslim north." The television program now reaches fifteen of the nineteen states in Nigeria, including a release in the northern states through which many Muslims see "Redemption Hour."

He had been told that as a black man he would never be accepted by the whites. Today he is greatly loved by white people in many parts of the world, and he has had successful crusades in the United States, Canada, Sweden, and Australia. Several white missionaries work under his direction, showing esteem and respect for his leadership.

Six months after Miracle Centre had been dedicated, the federal military government of Nigeria issued a decree that the building would be demolished—along with many other buildings—to allow for expansion of the Benin City airport. Benson was told the decree was irreversible. He went on television and declared, "If Miracle Centre is God's edifice, no man, no decree, no power can pull it down." A few months later the plan for the airport expansion was amended. Miracle Centre was left standing while more than thirty other buildings—including the traditional palace of an important official—were torn down.

He was told it would be impossible to maintain a constant building program without stopping. But since the first spade of dirt was turned to build Miracle Centre, Benson has not stopped building. After the Centre came the Bible school building, then a dormitory, then a headquarters office, then a missionary apartment building, then another dormitory, then the Women's Centre, then the television studio.

Still the fire burns in his bones, and the vision broadens. In 1977, Benson felt the Lord spoke to him a new word of direction: *"Take a step higher! I want a ministry for body, soul and spirit; I will tell you when to apply for land."*

The new direction is a university with a threefold emphasis: theology, medicine, and agriculture. It will be called Christian Faith University. In 1978 God helped Benson acquire forty-five acres of land by giving him favor with the villagers who owned the land, and with the local officials who had to approve the transaction. The land is paid for, and groundbreaking for the ten-million-dollar project was set for April 1, 1981. As always, there are those who say, "It cannot be done." But those words do not exist in Benson's vocabulary. He knows he has a word from the Lord, and that is the incentive that motivates him.

The first phase of the program—the school of theology—is already under way. The All Nations For Christ Bible Institute currently offers one year of training for ministry. As a follow-up to that year of resident study, a four-year program of extended study is offered with the International Correspondence Institute of Brussels, Belgium. It is called SEED—Seminary of Extensive Educational Development—with several pastors currently enrolled and working toward a B.A. degree.

The next phase will be the school of medicine, with the first building of the complex to be a clinic from which doctors and nurses will operate a program called "Operation Total Health."

---

The third phase will be a school of agriculture to provide training in a part of the world where the specter of famine seems always to hover near. Benson envisions bringing experts from other countries of the world to help establish Christian Faith University and train the Africans in these various fields. Like the existing Bible school, the university will draw students from other parts of Africa and beyond.

Benson declares. "God is going to give us a breakthrough and provide partners who have a vision to help with the expansion and outreach." He does not argue with those who think his plans are too big. He simply moves ahead with the workers God has given him who share his vision and his confidence that what God promises He will perform.

Over the years, a few dramatic experiences have motivated Benson and kept him on course in fulfilling God's call on his life. First was his conversion in 1960, when the fire of evangelism first began to burn in his bones. Then in 1968, the vision of the dead tree which came to life was the beginning of a new impetus in his ministry. Next was the miraculous manner in which God led him to find Missionary S.G. Elton and ask the older man to become his father in the Lord. And then came the prophetic word given when he was ordained by S.G. Elton and Gordon Lindsay, followed by his training at Christ For The Nations Institute, and God divinely leading him to "PTL Club," Charlotte, North Carolina. As a result of Jim Bakker giving Benson a large PTL Bible which he in turn, presented to the Governor of Bendel State, the governor ordered

1,000,000 Bibles for free distribution to all the schools in Bendel State.

Another significant event in Benson's life occurred on Sunday, May 31, 1981. The Word of Faith College conferred upon the Rev. B.A. Idahosa the degree of Doctor of Divinity, with all the rights, honors and privileges appertaining thereto.

Another memorable event happened in the capital city of the United States. Marion Barry, Jr., the mayor of Washington, D.C., wrote Benson a letter, welcoming him to the United States and to the nation's capital on the occasion of a luncheon given by the Interdenominational Ministerial Association for Community Concerns (IMACC) in Benson's honor. The mayor's letter read: "It is a special honor for Washington, D.C., to host your visit. While you are here, I hope you will have the opportunity to sample and enjoy the diversity of life and cosmopolitan nature of our metropolitan region and to visit the many famous historical monuments and unique attractions that are a part of our nation's capital. The residents of our city join with me in extending a warm welcome to you, and in wishing you a pleasant stay and a productive and enjoyable program."

Benson was ordained to the ministry in 1971. The scope of the work has grown to the extent that he presently oversees more than 600 churches throughout Africa. God called him to do the work of an apostle.

In November, 1981, ten years after his ordination to the ministry, another ordination service will be held. Conducted by Dr. David du Plessis, Dr. John L.

Meaves, Bishop Robert McAlister and other Christian leaders, this service will ordain Benson as a bishop.

Dr. Idahosa's United States headquarters is presently located in Washington, D.C. The office is called Africa for Christ, Inc. Workers there assist him with all the details concerning his ministering in different churches and before many groups in the United States.

After his first crusade in Benin City, and in the midst of criticism from local pastors who felt he was moving too far too fast, Benson had another linchpin experience. On May 18, 1973, the Lord awakened him at two-thirty in the morning and spoke these words:

*The world and its people are complaining daily of poverty and want. I have given you the mouth of miracles and blessings to my people. I have asked the cashiers of heaven to be on duty as long as you have a need for my own honor and glory. I shall supply all your needs according to my riches in glory* [Phil. 4:19].

*Begin to bless your people with all blessing; ask them to ask me anything they need, and I shall provide it for them. If only they will honor me with their wealth, I shall make them to be prosperous in all areas of their lives. I shall bless your partners and your co-workers.*

*Wake up, go to the church in the morning, and tell them poverty died last night. What you bless on earth is blessed in heaven. "Bless my people,"* says the Lord, who came to give the good life of abundance.

---

Many thousands of partners have caught the vision of Benson's work, and God has blessed them beyond measure. Truly, the future is as bright as God's promises.

Burn on, divine fire!

# Afterword

At the Benin City airport of Bendel State, Nigeria, the jetliner was packed with passengers. It had just begun to taxi toward the runway.

Dr. Benson Idahosa's Mercedes-Benz screeched to a halt in front of the plane.

Benson jumped out and waved his arms at the pilot.

The plane stopped.

The steps were lowered.

The captain stepped down and asked what the pastor wanted.

"I have two of God's important servants who must go to Lagos," Mr. Idahosa said.

"But we're loaded to capacity. Every seat is full," the captain explained.

"Never mind. Let me on board. They all know me; they see 'Redemption Hour' [Idahosa's weekly TV special]. Let me talk to them."

The man of God mounted the steps, walked down the crowded aisles—oblivious to everyone's annoyance. He was praying silently, believing for the right words. He returned to the front. Suddenly he whirled around. His eyes were slightly squinted—a "Benson Idahosa look" when he is discerning someone or giving a freshly inspired solution to an impossible problem.

"Excuse me, my friends. But I have two of God's special servants in my car. They must go to Lagos today [he jabbed the seat near him with this powerful forefinger] on this plane. Two of you will get off now so God's servants can board. God bless you!"

He waited a minute. No one moved. There was annoyed silence.

Benson walked the aisle again, looking, discerning. Then he pointed: "You, get up. You can go tomorrow!"

Then to the other side he signaled. "You, God bless you. Get up. You can travel later."

Both obeyed, gathered their belongings and followed the Bendel State preacher from the plane.

Just before descending the steps, Dr. Idahosa turned, raised his hands, and with tears in his eyes, praised the Lord and blessed the plane load of people. Then they all broke out in spontaneous clapping.

"God bless you all," Benson announced. "I'll see you on 'Redemption Hour' this Sunday evening." They clapped again, then Daisy and I boarded the jet for Lagos to meet our international flight from Johannesburg for France, England and the USA.

Benson Idahosa is more than a preacher. He is a pastor of over 10,000 people, a prophet of Bible faith and action, a counselor with miraculous, supernatural, God-given instincts for people's problems, a man with almost incredible answers for almost unbelievable problems, an apostle who walks with God and hears from God because he talks with God.

Dr. Idahosa is sought after by everyone in his state,

from government officials to beggars. When they pose their questions and explain their problems to this man, they expect a miracle solution, just as people did in Bible days with God's prophets. And the people get miraculous answers from this mighty leader.

Benin City respects and salutes this great man of God. I've been with him on visits to many officials, to the governor, to the powerful Benin tribal king. He moves with God, and his people know it.

His great miracle cathedral (his headquarters) seats over 10,000. More than a thousand churches have already been raised up under his leadership.

His International Bible School attracts upper-class people from eighteen African nations. And they come from Maurice, India, Pakistan, Bangladesh, Sri Lanka, Indonesia, Singapore, the Philippines, Hong Kong, Japan, Korea, the Middle East, Europe, England and other nations of the world—a truly international Bible training center of dynamic faith. People know that President Benson Idahosa practices what he teaches.

Dr. Idahosa's evangelistic ministry has carried him before multitudes of 100,000 and more, into nations around the world. He was the first black African evangelist to shake Australia in a massive crusade that got national attention.

His seminars are affecting Christians and church leadership in many nations.

I sincerely salute this man because he practices among his own people what he preaches to the world.

Benson Idahosa is a man who believes God's promises and God's miracle provisions apply to Africans as well as to Americans. He believes that if Africans plant in God's work, Africans will reap God's blessing.

Many who follow Pastor Idahosa's teaching have been saved out of poverty. They have learned the laws of sowing and reaping. They have learned to plant out of their desperate need and to look to God as their divine source, becoming prosperous Christians in their own land.

When Benson Idahosa was in Bible school, he read our books and discovered who he was (see chapter 11). This powerful realization of his own standing *with* God and *in* God and of the urgency of world evangelism, catapulted him from the ranks of the ordinary into world leadership as pastor, builder, counselor, prophet, teacher, apostle, evangelist—a man of godly wisdom and of Christ-like compassion whose ministry is blessing millions the world over.

*Fire in His Bones* is a dynamic story that will revolutionize readers' lives. The fire that burns in Benson Idahosa's bones will burn within you as you absorb the power, the anointing and the compassion of this man, Africa's greatest ambassador of apostolic Christian faith to the world.

T.L. Osborn
Tulsa, Oklahoma

Dr. Benson Idahosa's mailing address in the United States is:

Africa for Christ, Inc.
P.O. Box 1922
Washington, D.C. 20013
(202) 635-8422

In Nigeria you may write to him at:

Miracle Center
P.O. Box 60
Benin City, Nigeria
052 242 995

Special Christ For The Nations Edition of

# Fire In His Bones

## The Story of Benson Idahosa

This is the amazing account of what can be accomplished by one man who is totally dedicated to advancing the Kingdom of God in today's world. Benson Idahosa, who began from the first day of his conversion to share the gospel of Christ with everyone he met, continues to inspire all who meet him to attempt great exploits for the Kingdom.

The turning point in Benson's life came when the late Gordon Lindsay met him in Nigeria in 1971 and invited him to come as a scholarship student to Christ For The Nations Institute. In obedience to the Lord's leading, Lindsay had founded CFNI in 1970 as a bold step of faith. In the years since, thousands have entered the ministry as a result of the training received at the Institute. They continue to answer the call of the Great Commission, "Go ye into all the world . . ." (Mark 16:15).

Please write Christ For The Nations at the address below if you would like to receive any of the following:

A free subscription to CFN's monthly magazine.

Literature about Christ For The Nations Institute.

A complete list of Gordon Lindsay's books and CFN tapes.

Christ For The Nations
P.O. Box 24910
Dallas, TX 75224